ALASKA CHANCE

ALASKAN WOMEN OF CALIBER SERIES BOOK 3

MARYANN LANDERS

Copyright © 2022 by Maryann Landers

All rights reserved.

No part of this book may be reproduced in any form or by any electronic or mechanical means, including information storage and retrieval systems, without written permission from the author, except for the use of brief quotations in a book review.

All scripture quotations are taken from the Holy Bible, King James Version, KJV, public domain.

Quoted Hymn: Standing on the Promises, Public Domain.

Book Cover Design: Pro_ebookcovers, Fiverr

Editors: Jessica Martinez Copywriting and Editing Services and Kameo Monson Editing Services

Map image created and drawn by the talented Sonya Bitz of Tok Alaska. You can find her at

https://www.instagram.com/sonyabitzart/

❊ Created with Vellum

This book is dedicated to the Kelly, Briar and Crane families branching all over the country.
Mrs. N. Kelly, your faith in Christ is a testimony to the transforming power of one soul yielding to God, and bearing fruit from generation to generation.

PREFACE

This story was based on actual events except of course when they didn't happen and the people didn't exist. I may have muddled the time frame and changed elements for dramatic purposes.

CHAPTER 1

Ohio
December, 1963

Mary stirred her milkshake with an oversized straw and looked at me from across the table. The aroma of onion rings hung in the air at the diner where we'd met to discuss the details of my wedding. "I can't believe it's tomorrow. What else do you need on the guest tables?" she asked with an approving smile.

I peeked down at my pink strawberry shake, then up into her deep brown eyes. She shared such a powerful resemblance with her brother, James, who also happened to be my fiancé. Their dark features and friendly smile warmed every room they entered.

"Hello there, Sharon. Wake up." Mary waved as she spoke.

"Oh, yeah! Tomorrow." I touched my engagement ring and then spun it on my finger. "Seems like I've been planning the wedding for three years, not three months."

"Are you nervous?" Mary patted her dark-brown bouffant and her stiffened hair bounced at her light touch.

"Of course I'm nervous. I want it to be perfect. Well, better than perfect. Daddy has so much invested in my big day. It makes me sick to think about it."

"All right then, let's get back to business. Anything else for the guest tables?"

I leaned down to get my oversized tote bag and set it on the table. "Treat bags for the kids."

"You're kidding, right? Who makes treat bags for their own wedding?"

I shrugged. "I don't know. If I was a kid who had to sit through a wedding, I'd want a prize at the end." Between my fingers, I swirled one of the ribbons that I'd delicately tied on each of the cellophane-wrapped packages.

Mary touched my hand. "You're the epitome of thoughtful! Tell me, what's inside these cuties for the curtain climbers?"

"A few of my favorites: Lemon Heads, SweeTarts, an Astro Pop, and for a finale, a 100 Grand Bar. These kids hit the jackpot just for coming." I twisted in my chair and crossed my legs.

"Thank God, huh!" Mary exclaimed and tapped the table with her manicured fingernails.

My face flushed, and I placed a cool hand to my cheek. "Right." I averted Mary's gaze from my blush as I pulled another treat bag from my tote. "There's pink ribbon for the girls."

Mary waved her hand at me. "You're too much, Sharon. My brother doesn't deserve the sweet thing you are. A bride who serves an overdose of sugar to guests under three feet. You beat all." She rose straighter in her chair and leaned forward. "I'm looking forward to the dance after dinner. Maybe I'll get to do the twist with Bill. Are you wearing your light-blue Halston dress tonight?"

A smile spread across my lips. I glanced behind me, then looked back at my future sister-in-law. "I can't give away all my secrets, Mary."

"Okay, the bride is allowed one mysterious element. Just so

you know, it's no secret that the forecast calls for snow on your wedding day. Did you pack boots for your honeymoon?"

"Snow? How much?" I questioned, making a mental note to find my winter boots.

Mary tended to her stiff hairdo again. The amount of hairspray she used in a month was more than I did in a year. "I've no clue," she said. "Let's hope it's nothing like the storm that shut down Akron earlier this year. It took days to clear the turnpike. But a little snowflake here and there sounds awfully romantic to me."

"Your parents must have shown you kids what true love is, because both you and your brother are bent on it through and through." The milkshake gave me a chill, and I pulled my sweater up over my shoulders.

"Didn't yours?"

Not where I wanted my mind to drift. I bit my bottom lip and spun my mind. What to say with rose-colored glasses? I'd not seen as much overt affection in my childhood as other families had.

"In answer to your first question, there isn't anything else for the guest tables. Friends will arrive early and help decorate. I'm fussing over my veil in my spare time and doing my nails. There's packing to do, since I won't be returning to my apartment after the honeymoon." I slurped the last drops of my shake and dabbed my mouth with the napkin.

"Honey, take a break already. It's your rehearsal and dinner. Your nails can wait, and if you like, I'll take a peek at the veil." She inched forward in her chair. "Or you could go without."

My nails could wait? I scanned the tips of my pale fingers. Certainly, Mom would inspect them, I pasted a kind smile on for Mary. "All right, I'll wait to polish my nails until tomorrow, but I'll bring the veil for ideas. A shroud of purity is a must. I won't deny myself that."

Mary placed her leather handbag on her lap. She stroked the

sides of the kelly-green clutch. "C'mon, you must've shared some sugar with James."

"He's dreamy. But let's just say that tomorrow will be special, as it's intended to be. Heaven knows it's hard, but it's worth it." I've saved my whole heart for James. The next day, we'd usher in a lifetime of loving each other, and I was certain there would be adventure in our future. I'd follow him anywhere.

Mary and I each placed cash on the table and strolled out of the diner onto the streets of our quaint midwestern town.

AT THE DINNER PARTY FOLLOWING THE WEDDING rehearsal, James clasped my hands and stroked my ring finger, rubbing the solitaire diamond engagement ring like an eight ball for good luck.

"There's a ritual I'll want to share with you later," he said as he held my gaze. "It will determine our destiny."

Mesmerized by his touch, I blinked in hopes of clearing my mind. The band played Elvis' hit, *Can't Help Falling in Love*. James mouthed the chorus to me, melting me like an ice cream cone puddling in my palm on a hot summer's day.

Was there anything more exciting than marrying your true love? Two young lovers lost in each other, certain their devotion couldn't explode into anything more than it already had.

"Our destiny?" I asked, laughing. "Will I ever tame your innate passion for spontaneity? You know I like details. What's up your sleeve?" I spun my earring in place and then laid my hand on top of his.

His eyes widened. I'd played into his scheme with my questions. He'd teased, hoping to lasso me with a rope of curiosity. "Let's catch the dance so I can whisper sweet nothings to you.

I'll reveal the game later." He rose from the glass-topped table and held his hand out.

Yes, I'd succumbed to his plan.

We moved together, dancing to *I Only Want to be with You*, the popular Dusty Springfield song igniting memories from two years ago.

He'd asked me out on a date near Thanksgiving. Since I was already going with a guy, I'd declined.

As though he'd lingered in watchful waiting, he came to my door a few weeks after that relationship ended. His next invitation for a date was one I agreed to.

Four years my senior, he was ready for commitment, while I was still gawking at his fancy sports car. Our friendship blossomed faster than I'd ever imagined possible. It was so natural and easy to be together, I felt like fate had matched us.

Like a snowball taking on more and more snow with each roll, our love grew at an exponential rate, and we hurled forward toward marriage. We chose the anniversary of our first date for our wedding day. All part of our dream for a happily ever after.

As the dance wound down, James pulled me toward the edge of the dance floor. "I propose we play a little game of chance." He brushed my hair behind my ear as he spoke, and I felt his breath across my neck.

I swallowed and lingered in my response. "Oh?"

Still holding my hands, he took a step back and looked at me from head to toe. "By the way, you're stunning in that blue dress. Did Mary pick it out? I know she's thrilled to treat you as her pet, styling your hair and shopping for all the incidentals."

"Mary and I worked hard to think of everything." I brushed the front of my dress, looked up, and saw my dad strolling toward us. What held his gaze? Was my dress long enough? Maybe it was the choice of music? He drew closer, stopping short of bumping into James.

"Ahem."

My father's throat-clearing scheme worked, and James dropped his hold on me like a hot potato.

"Uh, yes, sir." James fumbled with his coat button and averted his eyes to the dance floor. "Were you wanting a dance with Sharon?"

Daddy brushed James off with a wave of his hand and took over the dance. "Move along, James, you're starting a lifetime of dancing in those shoes."

I bit my lower lip and scanned the room. Mom stood watching our every move. "Yes, Daddy. What is it? Did I leave out an important detail? Oh, is it the punch? Too sweet? I told Naomi to put in half the sugar. Uh, oh, not the cucumber salad! Did Laura put in that whole container of vinegar? I knew I shouldn't have wandered out of the kitchen to the dance so early." I let out a rapid fire of suggestions about what might've drawn his attention to me.

"Sharon, it's all delicious. I wanted a brief dance with my baby girl, then I'm off. You lovebirds can dance the night away." He searched my eyes. "Ready for tomorrow?"

My restless legs moved methodically to the music. "Yes. You've spared no expense for my dream wedding."

"I'm glad." He placed a soft kiss on the top of my head. "Good night, Ronnie."

A nickname of sorts for Sharon—perfect for someone who was supposed to the baby boy of the family. The constant reminder sank deep.

James and Mary huddled close at the corner of the room, lurking in the shadow of the low light as though they might pounce at any moment. Daddy turned to join Mom while my future husband scurried close with his sister in tow and waved me to follow. "C'mon Sharon, it's time."

CHAPTER 2

JAMES PULLED ME AWAY FROM THE DANCE TO THE oversized foyer. I drew my sweater higher on my shoulders, close to my neck, since the air was cooler away from the crowd and nearer the doors. "James, where are we going?" I asked.

He peered over his shoulder and lifted my hand in his.

A few of my cousins lingered near the front door, sharing a smoke, their laughter carried across the room with a chilly breeze. James moved to the coat-check closet and leaned against the wall, close to a small table. "My love, it's time for a Kline tradition." He rubbed his hands together. "We have some options, and I'd like to make a game of how we decide."

I scanned James' and Mary's faces for a clue. "I see. Options for what?"

"Options for us." James' smile spread across his entire face. "My family thrives on a whim and a whirl. Like I mentioned a couple of weeks ago, I put my name in for six different teaching jobs, all of them in different states. I heard from some last week, and then this afternoon, I heard from the rest." He took a pile of three-by-five cards from his sport coat's front pocket. "Klines leave major decisions to chance. Why not roll the dice and celebrate where we land?"

Mary's face beamed, assuring me it was not a joke. My heart beat faster, and I held my palm over my chest. Was this how we'd make all of our life decisions?

When we first met, I was drawn to his lighthearted approach. Early in our friendship, I'd taken into consideration that it would spill over into the ebb and flow of marriage; however, it didn't occur to me that there would be games involved.

"Wait, I almost forgot." Mary pulled an oversized cloth bag off her shoulder. "The blanket, James."

He put a hand to his forehead and shook his head. "I can't believe I let that slip. Everything in the right order. Place it on the table."

Mary spread the red velour cloth, smoothing the wrinkles.

"James, slow down." I placed my palm on his forearm. "More information."

"Yes, six cards, each with a state and job description. I'll give you bullet-point info and any tidbits I've collected along the way. Remember, we talked about these?"

"I know. Heaven knows it didn't occur to me you'd hear from all of them so soon and we'd need to pick one. Do you have to decide now?"

"No, but it's more fun this way."

I dabbed at my hair, checked my earrings, and then caressed my dress at my waist. Life with James would be an adventure. "Okay, fire away." I rubbed my sweaty hands together in nervous excitement.

As Mary pulled out the die and tossed it in her hand, James shuffled the cards.

I searched the room, watching other couples meander out from the dance and mingle near the door. If we moved, when would I see my family again? How far would we explore? And for how long?

James placed the first card on the table. "Number one is what

Chapter 2

I call small-town USA. Dubuque, Iowa. Rapid-fire facts are the following: teaching junior high, middle-class community, and over eight hours' drive from here. Climate isn't much different from us in Ohio." His eyes moved between Mary and me.

Was he looking for hints? I'd hold my card tight. No sense in attaching to a location right from the get-go.

"One word to describe your reaction please?" He held out his fist as though he had an invisible microphone for me to speak into.

I played along and leaned forward to talk into the mic. "Close."

"Thank you, ma'am. Next is not-so-small town USA. King of Prussia, Pennsylvania. Next door to Valley Forge where George Washington spent the winter with the Continental Army. A classic colonial backdrop. Job is high school level—multiple subjects—and requires additional training, but the school will provide it on campus. This option also includes housing. Again, the climate isn't much different from here, and the commute to visit family is roughly the same as Iowa. Your one-word response, please."

I smiled at James, who shuffled his feet back and forth. He'd make an excellent teacher, adding spice to any classroom. I clasped my hands in front of me and stated, "Historical."

"Mmm, I like that. You're lovely, Sharon." He moved closer and gave me a quick kiss on my cheek. "See, isn't this grand!"

Grand, but scary.

"Card number three is for a more drastic lifestyle change, taking on a one-room classroom in rural Kentucky. Backwoods, bluegrass, and most likely, the housing is an old farmhouse close to the property. Climate change would be minimal. Lifestyle—well, not sure on that one. Your word, my lady." James bowed to me with one arm across his abdomen.

I licked my lips, which held a straight smile. I'd play along. "Fried Chicken."

Mary joined in. "I love fried chicken. Still, I'm not too keen on the rural tone of that one. But I'm not the one moving."

"Rolling along, we have card number four. Downtown Fresno, California. I'd be teaching English as a second language to adults. We'd be on our own for housing. Known for a temperate climate, this locale is a few days' drive from Ohio." He leaned in, rubbing my shoulder, sending sparks up my neck.

"And my word is *tasty*." My mind lingered on the idea of living in the Golden State. I'd heard of the delicious grapes that grew there.

"Huh? All right, not sure what you mean, but that's okay." He shuffled the card to the bottom. "Number five is another jump, taking us to an international location in central Alberta, Canada. A small town outside of Edmonton called Fort Saskatchewan. Wheat and canola fields, cattle and country. There's housing provided for the small school. Climate is shockingly similar to Ohio, though it has longer winters and shorter summers."

"Another country? I don't remember this one." I raised my eyebrows.

"I tossed out the Texas offer and exchanged it for the Canada one. Sorry, I forgot to tell you. The Canadian prairie sounded more similar to here, and the job offer is substantially more money even with the exchange rate." James rubbed his fingers against his thumb, signaling more cash.

"My word for this mystery item is: *challenging*," I stated, unsure about the transplant to a new country.

Mary gave a spin, and the skirt of her dress twirled. "I'm so glad it's you and not me, Sharon! I can't imagine living in any of these places. Lord knows I love my boutiques and routine. But I'll come visit you."

I smiled at Mary's honest remark.

"Last, but not least in any way whatsoever, we have Fairbanks, Alaska," James said with a toothy grin.

Chapter 2

Mary's twirl stopped abruptly as she stared at James.

I blinked and swallowed hard at the lump rising in my throat. Where had this one come from?

I placed my hands on my hips. "James!"

He shrugged. "Okay, okay. I threw out the Florida one for this gem."

My mind spun. I'd have to explore a map to know for certain where the city was within the largest state in the Union. Any amount of reading I'd done about Alaska made it sound like another planet.

"Let me finish, ladies." James held out his hand like a stop sign. "Fairbanks is a golden opportunity involving teaching sixth grade. They laced the salary with benefits. The climate is arctic, but we'd live in the heart of a city dating back to the Klondike. Don't take time to think. Give me your gut reaction."

I didn't have to ponder for long. "Far out."

"I know, right? We're so lucky to have all these choices. Anywhere with you, my sweets." He grabbed my hand and held it over his heart. "This beats for you, and we're in it together."

Was there a right way to respond? I longed for more details of each spot and the time to read about and explore the possibilities. However, if we landed on one that I wasn't so keen on, it'd be a wasted effort. Seemed best to jump in feet first and find out more later. There'd be time. It was the middle of the school year. They couldn't possibly want us so soon. Several months of planning and packing would prepare us for a new trajectory in life. I know what James wanted me to say. His eyes pleaded with mine and searched my face.

I snapped my fingers and then pointed at him. "Let's roll."

He wiped at his forehead, dabbing pretend sweat. "Here you go." James motioned for Mary to take the die with a wave of his hand. "Give it a shake, and we'll take turns passing it around, but Sharon can cast the throw determining our destiny."

Even if we landed in an unfamiliar place, it didn't mean

forever. I was certain if we had this many options to begin with, over time, there'd be more. How many places would we explore?

James laid the cards out one at a time on the red blanket spread across the table. "We have Iowa, Pennsylvania, Kentucky, California, Alberta, and Alaska."

Mary shook the cube in her folded hands and blew on the die. After a few shakes and a kiss to the top of her hands, she tossed it at James, who gave a whoop of delight.

"Come on, lucky dice. I won't say what I'm hoping for." He shook the die and did a little jig in place.

I closed my eyes for a moment and shook my head. This evening would be ingrained within my mind for the rest of my life. James dancing, the die rolling, and our first adventure taking root. He stopped and held my hands, then opened my clasped palm and placed the warm die inside.

"Here, my sweets. It's all yours."

There wasn't a way to cross my fingers and shake the die. I chanted over and over in my mind.

Please let it not be Alberta or Alaska. Not Alberta or Alaska.

Mary smoothed the red blanket repeatedly and then rubbed her hands together.

I shook one more time, then tossed the die onto the fabric of fate. We leaned in to read the number.

A six for Alaska.

James reached for my hands and drew me to him. He picked me up by my waist and spun me in the air.

Feeling dizzy from the spinning, I laughed out loud at the moment and at the idea that we were launching our life together to the literal ends of the earth. Why not take a chance on Alaska? What was there to lose?

CHAPTER 3

The sunshine glared off the windows of the countryside chapel on the hill. The white steeple rose loftily, and my gaze followed to its tip, pausing on the cross at its peak. Would being married in a church bring me the good luck I yearned for? I'd heard of other couples struggling in their marriages, tirelessly striving for peace. Was I prepared to promise James forever?

My brother John cleared his throat, and I glanced over at him in the driver's seat, his hands resting on the steering wheel as he turned off the car. "Well, Ronnie, it's my last chauffeur ride. Ready to usher in a life of riding shotgun with James?"

Although John had pestered me growing up, I'd noticed his care for me these last couple of years, and he'd been faithful to check in and pick me up for coffee regularly. Maybe now he didn't mind the little sister I was, instead of the brother he'd wanted.

I looked at his soft-blue eyes, and they drew me to answer honestly. "Probably not ready, but I'm diving in."

John set his hand on my shoulder and gave it a light squeeze.

A tear formed in my eye, and I rubbed it with the tip of my

finger, careful not to smudge my makeup. "Thanks for the drive. I'll miss our outings."

How was I going to say goodbye to him next year when we moved?

"Miss our outings? Why? I'm not going anywhere. You're getting married, Sharon, not traveling to the moon." John shifted in his seat.

"James accepted a job offer in Alaska. It might as well be outer space." No sense in holding back the news.

I held my breath, waiting for John to banter a response. Surely, he'd give us the worldly wisdom he always dished out, always wanting to steer me in the right direction.

"That sounds outstanding."

I blinked back tears and spun my ring, then inhaled and smiled in return at his enthusiasm. "It's definitely going to be different than living here. When we get back from our honeymoon, I'm sure we'll have more details." I touched John's hand, feeling the warmth of his palm. "Thanks for the ride."

"Of course. I'll bring your things in from the back. Alaska. Man, I've always wanted to go there." John shook his head and opened his door.

I stepped out and gathered my purse from the seat.

"Boots?" John held up my oversized winter boots, which I'd set on the back floor.

"Yes, the forecast is for snow." I gazed up at the blue sky and shrugged.

"It's just like you, Ronnie—to be ready for anything," John said.

"YOUR VEIL TURNED OUT BEAUTIFULLY, MY DEAR." My mom tugged the fabric down my neck somewhat harder than I thought necessary. Her hands bounced off the shroud it created over my hair. "My veil was much longer. My mom told me, 'cover as much as you can; don't leave room for minds to wander.' Yours is a little short, but it'll do."

The woman in the mirror stared back at me. Was that fear in her eyes? Yes, but not fear of getting married. A closed smile crossed her face, showing me that she'd learned how to please others close to her.

Yes, Mom. For you, Mom. Please just say it's all wonderful so I can enjoy the day.

I reached back to touch my mom's hand resting on my shoulder. "Thanks."

"There you are!" Mary's voice carried across the room. "I have some beverages in the kitchen down the hall if you'd like. Guests are trickling in."

My mom touched the small of my back with one hand and placed the other on my stomach. "There you go, stand tall."

I nodded in reply to Mary, and she gave me a wink. My mom turned to walk away, saying, "I'll go find your dad."

My eyes closed. I teetered in place and reached for my soon-to-be sister-in-law.

Mom's heels clamored in the hall, echoing in my ears, and Mary grasped my elbow. "Sharon! Breathe!"

Mary whisked a nearby chair under me, and I plopped down. Her hand fanned my face, and I blinked rapidly, then opened my eyes.

"I'll get you a sip of water," Mary said. "Now sit here, and I'll be back in a flash."

I ached to see the day through, to see that the hard work of planning had paid off and everyone was happy. I didn't want to fail anyone. I inhaled, pursed my lips, and held my breath. I exhaled and placed my hands on my thighs. The soft fabric of my dress touching my fingers brought me to reality.

I'm moments from my wedding.

"Sharon." Mary's voice carried into the room before she

entered. I lifted my head and smiled at the sight of her. She held a glass of water in one hand and a pitcher in the other. "I brought you choices. A little or a lot?"

I stood and reached for the glass. "I'll take a little. Thanks, sis."

"Oh, I like that." She waved at me. "You're welcome, sis. I glimpsed the groom. He looks a tad nervous." Mary's giggles eased the tension that'd crept up my neck.

I swallowed the cool water and set the cup down on a nearby table. "Your brother has the flowers in the kitchen," Mary said. "He'll make sure the guys have their boutonnieres, then bring our bouquets. I'm so glad you kept the day simple, yet elegant."

I gave my cheeks a pinch and followed the gesture with a smile that spread across my face. "There isn't anything that can spoil the day, sis. We're set."

Daddy entered the room and reached his arms out to me. His handsome features radiated from the three-piece suit that he brushed gently before embracing me. "My girl." His hug lingered. "You're beautiful, Sharon."

"Thanks, Daddy." I looked down at my shoes sparkling in the light. Every detail, no matter how small, from my shoes to my hairpins, had been noted and checked repeatedly in hopes of a smooth wedding.

"Did you notice outside, Ronnie? It's snowing." His powerful arms spun me around to the back of the room, where a frosted window centered the wall.

What? Snow? The weather-guessers were right. I moved to squint through the pane but couldn't make out the size of the flakes or how heavily they fell. Was snow a blessing from above or an omen of doom? "I like the snow," I said. "It's fine. I'll still be carrying a bouquet of radiant flowers and…oh, Daddy, is there something else I need to do because of the snowstorm? I brought boots for me, but I never…"

"Ronnie." He clasped my face with his hands. "Let's wait over here. When John brings the flowers, it's go time. A little snow never hurt no one." He gently took my hand and placed it on his forearm.

THE MINISTER PAUSED AFTER WE HAD SAID OUR VOWS and a wide grin spread across his face. "By the power vested in me, I now pronounce you Mr. and Mrs. James Kline." He leaned forward, closer to James. "You may kiss your bride."

I glanced at the minister, then to James, who beamed widely. He reached to draw my veil back, and his kiss melted any frozen icicles of worry that had formed within my thoughts about the whirling snow outside. "I love you, Mr. Kline," I whispered in his ear.

He grabbed my hand as I reached to take my bouquet from Mary, and we marched down the aisle. I gave sparkling smiles to the guests as we passed. I glanced over my shoulder at my parents, who stood to follow us, along with the wedding party.

James gave a little tug as we stopped near the gift table. How'd a wedding go by so fast after all the hours it took to plan and prepare?

"Remember, we wait here and greet the guests," James stated matter-of-factly.

Our wedding party followed in formation for the receiving line.

"I hope someone will find a glass to clink so I can give you a smooch," he stated with a curled smile on his lips.

"James!"

He grabbed my hand and gave it a squeeze. "One can wish."

My parents came, following our lead, and reached to hug me first.

"Beautiful, it was magnificent." Mom's words echoed in the small space.

"And my *beautiful* wife and I are pleased to announce to you both that we're moving to Alaska," James announced.

Without missing a beat, he shook the hand of my uncle, who stood close behind my dad.

I tried to concentrate as we embraced the wedding guests one by one. Throughout the time spent in the reception line, I hoped that blurting out the news was the best way to announce our move, as opposed to mulling it over while chewing tender roast beef during a Sunday family dinner.

Mary tipped forward in line and waved her bouquet at me. "Sharon, did you see all the snow? Maybe it's fates' way of telling you Alaska is beckoning you to hurry."

Hmph, no way. The move was going to be paced like a well-planned, five-course meal.

James leaned over and pulled my veil back a little farther. His whisper ticked my ear. "I hope the snow doesn't keep us from getting to our honeymoon location. It might not be as fun if I have to give you a piggyback through the drifts."

I stood on my tiptoes and gave him a quick kiss.

"I'm ready, James Kline. For richer or poorer, snow drift or sand dune, I'm yours."

James let out his typical whoop.

We were ready for our forever.

CHAPTER 4

Earlier in the morning, Mary picked me up and pleaded with James to let me go with her for a few hours. I'd been enjoying the coffee in hand and cuddles on the couch, and I hesitated in my response 'cause it had been a while since I'd time alone with Mary. After arriving home from our honeymoon, James and I spent a good bit of time unpacking some things and setting up our apartment together.

Now, I went from store to store with Mary at the shopping mall. "James suggested a *few* warm things," I stated, as the screech of the metal hangers on the wardrobe pierced my ears and I winced at the noise.

"I have a different definition of *a few*, my dear. Winter clothes go on clearance now, in January. Load up the cart!" Mary threw a bright red sweater in and plucked a yellow tunic off a hanger and held it up to herself. "It's too cute to pass up. I'm glad James thought you should come shopping with me."

Mary stepped closer. "Did you get all your gifts opened?"

I scanned the store, then looked into her eyes, which were wide with curiosity. "Not quite."

"What? I'd have ripped those puppies open already. What's holding you back?"

I blushed at her comment and smiled. "Mary, there's no rush. We're savoring it. Writing thank you cards and..."

She stood behind me, placed her hand on my shoulder, and turned me to face her. "Ah, I get it. And a little kissing. Guess it's expected." Mary spun on her heels. "Just curious what things you may have received as gifts."

"I tell you what, why don't you come inside when we get back, and you can help us finish unwrapping the rest? Having you write names of who gave which gift would be helpful."

I'd mentioned the need to finish unwrapping gifts to James earlier in the week, and we'd put it off. How did the short days of January leave me with so little energy to consider larger tasks? James figured the stress of the wedding had weighed me down and now that it was over, my body was recuperating.

"Afterward, we can do some baking," I said.

Mary dropped the dress in her hand into the cart. "Baking?"

"I've been meaning to make a little something for our neighbor lady. She gathered our mail while we were on our honeymoon."

Mary gave me a side hug and pushed the cart forward. "Like I said before, you're sugar and spice and everything nice. Let's go tear into those gifts."

When Mary and I returned from taking the cake we'd made to the neighbor, we found a note propped up on the kitchen table. I read it aloud. "'Gone hunting.' I wonder what that means?"

I washed my hands at the sink, turning the water all the way to hot as I reached for the kettle.

Mary placed our shopping bags on the couch. "You'll get good at deciphering his code talk. Though, I've known him all my life and I'm still not there yet."

Chapter 4

"Would you like some coffee?" I filled the kettle, then placed it on the stove.

A piping hot drink sounded heavenly. The wind blew fiercely outside, and the short walk to the car and into the apartment had left a chill running down my back.

Mary walked over and opened the cupboards, digging around. "We're sisters now. I'll just help myself. No need to wait on me." She opened one cupboard, then another. "Where do you keep your cups? Never mind, I'll keep looking until I find them."

Mary found herself a mug and set it on the counter. After placing a fist on her hip, she reached for my hand. "Sharon, I keep forgetting to ask you—What did your parents say about Alaska?"

The silence falling from James' statement at our wedding had resonated like a brisk breeze off lake Erie. Truth be told, we hadn't talked about it again.

"Nothing." I eased my hand out of Mary's and opened the coffee canister, still out from that morning.

Mary opened the fridge and pulled out the carton of half-and-half. "I'll need a little help here since I don't know them well. Is that good or bad?"

"Hard to say. After the wedding, we whisked ourselves away for two weeks. We've hardly been back. I haven't been to their place yet, so we haven't really talked about it."

Were we avoiding the encounter? I couldn't deny that I was curious about their thoughts. Did they discuss the move over tea in the evening? Or brush it off, not taking us seriously?

A rattle of the front doorknob startled me, and I turned to see James come in. "My beautiful bride." A smile spread across his face as he walked to me. "Hey, Mary."

I leaned in for James' kiss and wrapped my arm around his waist. "Brr, your coat is cold." I pulled away and placed my arms around myself. "Now, tell me, what were you *hunting* for?"

James removed his gloves and rubbed his hands together.

"I'm so glad you asked." His dark eyes danced, and he looked from Mary to me. He grabbed my hands and held them to his chest. "I was out hunting for an extra coat."

Would I ever get used to his playful character? He challenged my ingrained sense of order. "Oh, and did you find one?" I searched his face for a clue. Was he holding something back?

"No, and now I know I'll have to hunt more when I get to Alaska in four months." His eyes widened, and he raised his dark eyebrows.

I blinked rapidly to absorb what he'd said. "Four months?" Again, I'd played into his lure of surprise. "You mean seven months, right?"

Surely, he'd stumbled on his words. I stepped back and turned off the kettle that whistled on the stove.

"No, my love," he said as he leaned on the kitchen counter.

Mary moved from the kitchen over to our small living room. "Don't mind me, I'll just take cover over here. And I'll get the coffee ready in a minute."

James explained. "After you left, the school district called. They need me to come sooner. We might as well take the polar plunge instead of waiting." James closed the gap between us.

How did our fairytale adventure turn sour in my gut? I put my hand on my belly. "We've hardly had time to swallow the news of a job offer, and now we're leaving?"

"Sharon, it'll all come together. Did you find some warm clothes? You're going to need them."

I nodded, even though I'd barely heard him.

"Okay, good. Let's do something to take our minds off it for a bit."

"Yeah, like opening these gifts." Mary spoke up from the living room, where she sat curled up on the couch. "I can hardly wait."

James gave my forearms a gentle squeeze before he released his grip. I willed myself to speak. "All right."

Chapter 4

I let the concept of Alaska take root in my mind. Maybe James was right—just dive in feet first instead of anticipating it for several months.

"I'll get these beauties all lined up for you," said Mary.

I glanced over and caught the nod between her and James.

Mary clapped her hands. "I love opening presents. I'm going to have to find myself a guy so I can get married and be surrounded by ribbons and bows."

I brushed my tunic with my hands as I made my way to the living room. James patted his lap, and I moved to him. We were in this together. Hadn't we determined to let fate carry us? And here we were, floating on the Alaskan dream of snowflakes and mountains.

"First"—Mary placed a large box on the coffee table—"open this beast. I can't believe you let it taunt you in the corner. It's massive."

A silver ribbon on top of the gift glistened in the light. "Go ahead, Mary, I know you want to." James cleared his throat and rubbed my back.

Mary squealed and tore into it like she was starving for food and the gift held her next meal. "Oh, it'll be amazing."

I rested my head on James' shoulder and smiled at Mary as she ripped at the gift wrap.

"Why didn't you invite the family to come and watch you open gifts? Isn't it tradition?" Mary pulled at the tape holding the box together at the top. It didn't budge.

"It is," I said. "But it felt like a private moment to me. After all the fanfare of the wedding, I wanted to take my time with each gift." I looked at James, who returned my smile.

Mary pulled at the tape again and fell backward as it broke loose. We erupted with laughter, and she bounced up, digging into the box. "You should see me at Christmas and birthdays. I'm relentless."

I dabbed my eye where a tear had formed from laughing. "It might be more fun watching you open all our gifts."

She tugged at a box wedged inside the larger box. "What in the world? Ugh, it's hard to get out." Mary tipped the larger box sideways.

I got up from the couch and helped her pull the smaller box out, then sat down next to James.

"A hostess trolley. These are divine." Mary rubbed the side of the box with her hand.

"Interesting." James' one-word answer summed it up.

How would these gifts fare on a trip north?

"I'll move it over here." Mary slid the box over. "I have my eye on this other one over here." She reached for a smaller gift wrapped in sparkling gold wrap with an oversized bow on top. "Looks like a treasure beckoning to be discovered. Here, you two can unveil this one." Mary placed a gift next to James and me on the couch.

I pulled the bow off and placed it on James' head. He rolled his eyes.

"You're the best gift of them all," I said, before leaning in to give him a peck on the cheek.

Together, we pulled at the wrapping. Inside was a small cardboard box without a label.

"Here, go ahead." James handed it to me.

I opened the end and slid out a frame. I held it out to see what was cross-stitched on the canvas.

Mary read it aloud.

"Trust in the Lord with all thine heart; and lean not unto thine own understanding. In all thy ways acknowledge Him, and He shall direct thy paths."

"Huh, I haven't heard that one before. You have a religious friend or something?" Mary reached for the frame, and I handed it to her. She looked at the back of it and then at the front again. "Kind of a chintzy frame. Guess it'd look okay in the hallway if you like that sort of thing." She held her hand to her mouth. "I'm sorry. This is why you didn't unwrap these in front of people." She handed the gift back and folded her hands in front of herself. "I'll grab some paper and write them down."

I stole a glance at James and winked. Mary chattered while we continued to unwrap our generous gifts. The frame with the Bible verse leaned against the coffee table. While reading a card, I glanced at the embroidered words. Trust the Lord? Don't lean on your own understanding, and He'd guide you? It was like a foreign language to me.

What would trusting God look like? We'd tossed the dice and left our future to chance. So far, so good. How long did it take for God to answer if you waited on Him instead of chance?

Someone had put time into the gift, so I hesitated to place it in the closet with the other pictures gifted to us. Would it be wrong to box up a Bible verse gift and put it in a drawer only to pull it out for show when the gift-giver came for dinner?

"Hey there, daydreamer?" Mary waved her hand at me. "You need a nap, don't you? I'll see you two love birds later when I come back for the cup of coffee I didn't have yet. Thanks for letting me join in the fun."

"Thanks for the visit, Mary." I rose and walked Mary to the door and gave her a hug goodbye.

Turning, I scanned the full living room. So much for setting up the apartment. Now to figure out what to do with all these wedding gifts. As I picked them up, I stumbled at the image of my parents pacing the living room at the news.

How will I tell them we're leaving before summer?

CHAPTER 5

THE CLANGING OF MY MOM'S SPOON ON HER TEACUP took on a rhythmic tempo. Her eyes followed the spoon's motion, and the idea of watching the tea spin in her cup brought a nauseating feeling to my stomach. I moved my gaze to Daddy, whose clasped hands rested on the table.

I gulped and swallowed before I spoke. "We'll leave mid-May."

The notebook on the table next to me held all the information I had about our move. Would having all the details written down bring peace?

Mom's spoon ceased its clinking, and she set it down on her china saucer. "Sharon, it's so sudden. Would you consider letting James go ahead of you to make sure the move will suit you both and then joining him later?"

I'd be lying to say doing just that hadn't been a consideration, but I'd avoided lingering on it. "I'll go where he goes." *Was I too abrupt?* Surely, they must admire my commitment to my new husband.

Daddy coughed, then leaned back in his chair. "Tell me, Ronnie, what's it like in Fairbanks in May?"

His question caught me off guard. "Uh, I don't know. I'm

assuming it's still cold. I've yet to read much about it. We've been opening gifts, putting things away, and now this. I'll need to pack soon, and maybe leave some boxes here if it's okay."

Daddy's attentive eyes searched mine, and then a smile grew across his face. Did he approve? He spoke each word with ease. "Sure, and don't worry. You'll figure it all out."

"We won't be close by to help. You'll be on your own, Sharon." Mom's declaration sent an icy chill up my neck and into the base of my head.

On my own. When had I ever been on my own?

"We'll be a phone call away," said Daddy. "I'll be curious to hear all about it and look forward to your return next summer over break." He pushed his hands down onto the table to brace himself as he stood up. "More tea, my dear?"

Mom picked up her spoon and stirred her tea again. "No, thanks."

"Hey there," my brother called out as he came through the front door. "Hi, Ronnie. What's up? Did someone die? Why the sad faces?"

"It's all good, son. Ronnie was telling us about Alaska."

"Ah, yeah. I can't wait to go visit next year." He placed his hands on my shoulders and gave them a squeeze.

My mom cleared her throat. "She's leaving in May."

"Right on. Even better. Need help with anything?"

Thank God for my brother. I sat up straighter and picked up my notebook. "I'm headed home to pack some boxes. If you'd like to help with those…?"

"Sure." He spun on his heels and as quick as he'd zipped in, he turned to leave. "See you, Mom and Dad."

I pushed in my chair and looked at both of my parents. Would I ever attain their approval? Even now, as a married woman cutting the apron strings, was that possible?

My mother stood up and gave me a tepid smile. "Thanks for

coming, Sharon." Her voice barely carried over the noise her chair made as she pushed it close to the table.

My dad waved as we walked out of the kitchen.

My brother whistled as he strolled around our apartment. His carefree ways were obvious to all who met him. How did he perform the ritual so well? those necessary dance steps to avoid Mom's critical eye? She beamed in his presence. Did he remind her of someone?

I'd conjured a story in mind as I listened to him whistle while packing a few small boxes in the kitchen. Mom had lost a brother when she was little. Her eyes had always glazed over the few times she spoke of him.

I closed my eyes and dug into the deep memories. Her brother was young and curious and wandered from the safety net of her care. I'd many, many assumptions I believed were true of how she blamed herself. How else can you explain her brisk brush of recollection? She must blame herself.

"Ronnie?" John's call startled me, and I jolted in place, catching the box as it fell from my hands.

I placed the box on the floor. "Oh, sorry."

"Where do you want me to put these fancy dishes?"

I brushed the stray hair from my cheek. "Good question. It's all happening so fast. I barely unpacked them."

I rubbed my hands together. Time to put some elbow grease into labeling the boxes and organizing them.

"Are you okay?" John walked over to me and placed a hand on my shoulder.

"Yup." I swallowed, then looked up to search John's eyes. "It was the luck of the dice, you know. What were the chances we'd end up going north to our future? Promise you'll come see us?"

John reached for the box at my feet. "Absolutely."

James called out as he walked in the door. "Hey!"

"Hi, honey!" I stepped into the entry to give him a kiss hello. We'd vowed to greet each other with at least a peck.

He wrapped me in a hug, then turned to the kitchen.

"Just in time to help us pack," I said.

James and John bantered over the latest sports news as I placed some of our delicate kitchen items in tissue paper. I traced the freesia petals on a teacup. The lemon-scented flower was a favorite garden blossom from my mom's perennial beds. What flowers would I see in Alaska? Good grief, did flowers even grow in the arctic? I laid the cup on one saucer, tucked neatly under protective wrapping.

Had the snow showers on our wedding day been a warning? Could they have been a shroud of prophecy? James' and John's voices grew louder, and their laughter resonated their haphazard ways amid the winter storm brewing in my core.

I needed one more item to fill the box. I searched the area, then sauntered over to the living room. On the coffee table was the slight frame with the scripture verse embroidered on it. I smiled in remembrance of us opening our wedding gifts.

Later that evening, James had played one of his unique word games and coined several nicknames for the scripture frame, including *legacy lettering* and *mayhem monograms*.

I carried the frame to the kitchen, set it face down on top of the china, and taped the cardboard flaps shut, writing the number on the side of the box that corresponded with my index-card listings. There was a certain satisfaction that came with the small task of cataloguing the few household goods we'd collected.

CHAPTER 6

ALAN HIGHWAY
May, 1964

My red wool Simonetta coat wrapped around me like a protective cocoon. I'd curled myself in, pulling in my arms and elbows to hold the warmth close to my core. My sleeves hung lifeless at my sides, and I looked down at the ugly military-surplus footwear I'd traded my knee-high go-go boots for. We'd left the warmth of mid-May weather in Ohio for the cool, brisk winds of the Rockies, and now the chilly nights of the Yukon Territory. Was I going to acclimate to the northern extreme? I'd prided myself on my bravery of Ohio winters, and already I was chilled from our nights of camping. The farther north we traveled, the more sunshine we enjoyed, but the night temperatures were far from the eighty-degree temperatures we'd left behind.

I put my arms in my sleeves and inserted the receipt from the gas station in my note bag. I dug around for the pen I'd placed in it earlier. We'd enjoyed journaling our trip and recording the campgrounds we'd tented at, the morning and evening temperatures, and the towns where we'd topped off our gas tank.

"What's got your tongue this morning?" James glanced at me

Chapter 6

from the corner of his eye while maintaining close attention to the road.

"Oh, I'm sorry. Just amazed at how far we've come." Not really a white lie. I scanned the road ahead of us. Each bump of gravel reminded me that we'd traversed over a thousand miles already.

"That's not what I thought you'd say. You have a sad look in your eyes. I wondered if you were missing home?"

Missing home? It hadn't crossed my mind. "More like wondering what my parents are thinking."

"You need to try and let that go." James placed a hand on my shoulder.

I bit at my lip, recoiling at the thought of my mom's countenance as we'd said goodbye. Her eyes sullen and moist while she flooded me with questions I couldn't answer.

The jolt of the car screeching to a halt shook me. "James!" I spoke too loudly and braced myself on the dash.

He pointed into the ditch. "There's a moose!"

"Good land! Did you have to slam on the brakes?" My terse tone set the mood, and I gulped back my reaction.

"Well, sor-ry. I happen to be enthralled with every animal I see." James moved the vehicle forward with rapid acceleration.

My hands continued to grip the dashboard. "It's not your sports car, sheesh."

"Where did my supportive wife disappear to?" James pretended to scan the roads and glanced over each shoulder.

Did he think his joke would lighten the mood?

My irritation shocked me. I was a team player, and I enjoyed his playful appreciation for most everything. What was going on with me?

I knew the answer. There had been too many hours of silence, and I'd let my musings wander back in time, dwelling on my past efforts to please my parents.

I pulled my boots off, tucked my feet under me, and rubbed

my cold toes. "I'm sorry, James." The tug deep inside me to make it right had risen to the surface.

"I'm sorry too, sweets." His hand moved to my knee, and he gave it a little squeeze. "I've been waiting for our first lovers' quarrel. Phew, glad we got it out of the way." He wiped his brow and shook his hand as though brushing invisible sweat from his head.

I couldn't help the smile spreading across my lips. I unbuckled my seat belt and slid over to him, setting my head on his shoulder. "James?"

"Yeah?"

I blurted out my question with rapid speed. "Is there any part of you that isn't so sure about Alaska? Like being way up there, so far away from what is familiar?"

His hand rubbed my shoulder. "Mmm, nope."

My sarcasm sprouted. "Nice long, drawn-out male response." I looked out the window. "A simple, 'nope.' Is there an emotional thermometer tucked in there?" I gave his side a jab.

"The only thing that matters is my gauge for you, and you rev it through the roof." He whooped and squeezed me in.

Later in the evening, by flashlight, I'd journal my own impressions of the move. I'd leave James aside with his fairytale elation and divulge my emotions to my yellow tablet. I closed my eyes and let the jostling of the vehicle sway me like I was being lulled to sleep in a hammock.

WE STOPPED AT THE AMERICAN–CANADIAN BORDER crossing and sat wide-eyed at the top of the hill, looking down into the valley below. There was no real fencing protecting the Canadian and Alaskan border, simply a line of trees that extended as far as the eye could see in both directions. No stark

Chapter 6

contrast differentiated one side from the other since there wasn't a community in the remote location.

James opened his door and got out. Then, as though an earthquake had erupted under his feet, he leaped forward and rushed to my door, pulling me out of the car and grabbing onto my hand.

"What are you doing?" I asked as he tugged me over to the other side of the road.

He picked me up in his arms and stood next to the geographical markers for Canada and the United States. "I'm going to carry you over the threshold from one country to the next."

With me in his arms, James leaped from one side to the other.

"James! You're going to drop—"

We tumbled to the ground on the United States side of the border marker and fell hard. Our laughter exploded, and I landed with my head on his chest.

"—me!"

His whole body shook with glee, and we were breathless, cackling.

James lifted up my head with his hands, and we sat up. He planted a kiss on my lips. "Welcome to Alaska, sweets."

"Thanks."

We'd fallen in to our new home after a week of camping and jostling down the narrow, gravel roads. Had we plummeted to our destiny of adventure? Or did our tumble foreshadow a downward spiral of adversity?

CHAPTER 7

Fairbanks

September, 1964

Our first few months in Fairbanks, we settled into our apartment and a usual routine. We'd walk the streets in the evenings, taking our usual route and enjoying a typical night's banter. It was mostly fun, but also biting, with the night air sending chills through the layers I wore. James was invigorated by the walks in the cooler temperatures, while I was climatizing by the drastic differences between Alaska and Ohio.

The city was much more civilized than I'd imagined, especially after the hundreds of miles of boreal forest we'd traversed to arrive. The buildings were a mix of modern and iconic, reflecting the Klondike era the city was known for.

Almost everyone we met was buzzing over the earthquake that had rocked Alaska on Good Friday, in March, earlier in the year. The grocer told us her story, as did the mailman and the kids who played on the corner. I was certain it affected most people in one way or another. If not them, then someone they knew.

The city's motto, *Fairbanks, Alaska's Golden Heart*, suited the culture of the folks we'd met. We'd both commented on the

Chapter 7

friendly welcome we'd received from strangers when they heard we were from the *lower forty-eight,* a common term in Alaska for the continental US.

One brisk September evening, James and I held hands as we walked on Lacey Street. Another young couple strolled toward us and waved.

"I feel famous here," James announced as he swung my arm extra high.

"I guess it's what happens when you visit with every stranger you meet on a simple walk."

James loved the group dynamics, where I preferred to engage with people one-on-one.

"Mmm," he said as he slowed his arm movement.

Our hands were still intertwined, but did I sense that he wanted to pull back?

"Hey, let's go see a show!" James pointed to the Lacey Street Theatre on the corner.

"A show? This late?" I questioned his spontaneity again. "What's showing?"

"Let's look." We stopped and scanned the signs out front.

Does he expect me to want to join in his every interest and whim?

He dropped my hand and threw his arms in the air, announcing, "*The Incredible Mr. Limpet*! I wanted to see it. I've heard it's a real gas! Don Knotts is the best."

I didn't share his enthusiasm for war movies. "Mary Poppins is showing as well." I pointed out.

James looked at me from the corner of his eye. "Kidding?" The inflection in his voice rose with the question.

The familiar nag in my stomach reminded me that I was not abiding by my initial newlywed commitment of aiming to please. "No, I wasn't joking. I've heard it's endearing."

James pretended to gag himself. "Sharon, it's a musical!"

I narrowed my stance and tightened my peacoat around my

waist. "I love music. In fact, I've been thinking of finding lessons at the university to brush up on my piano."

"Deal." He grabbed my hand before I could answer. "*You* bask in piano lessons, and *we* feast on war movies. Let's try the musical next time. Okay?" He placed money on the cashiers' counter for the show and tugged me to follow.

THE NEXT MORNING, I SCRAMBLED SOME EGGS ON THE stovetop while the coffee perked. I brushed strands of hair from my face, tucking them back. These early mornings, seeing James off to work, gnawed at me with an intense exhaustion. My mode was late night and James' was early morning. Not only did he spring out of bed, but he did so with gusto and desired a team effort on my part. My senses didn't awaken until the caffeine settled in and pushed out the languor deep inside. How was I going to sustain this effort all school-year long?

"Good morning, sweets." James sauntered into the kitchen and placed his arms around my waist. He kissed my neck under my ear and lingered.

His touch tingled my skin, and I smiled. "Good morning. Coffee is almost ready."

"Groovy. So, what are you up to today?" At the cupboard, he pulled out a mug.

I stirred the eggs with the spatula. The job search had been tedious, but I had a new lead to share. "Huh, *groovy* you say!" I raised my weary eyebrows. "I have an interview at the TV station."

"TV?" James turned to stare at me with wide eyes.

Ah ha, I had him! "Yes." I continued to stir the eggs, hoping to pique his interest.

"Do we need to play twenty questions?" James reached for the coffee percolator on the stove.

Chapter 7

"Sure!"

"C'mon, I'll be late for work. Tell me." He gave me a little jab at my side with his finger.

"I'm interviewing to be the star of the show!" I opened my arms out wide and grinned at him.

"Okay?" James narrowed his eyes at me, searching my face.

I laughed out loud and gave in. "Gary told me to apply at the office to run the kids' program."

Gary was our landlord and also the TV station manager.

"Really? The kids' program? I'm not familiar with that one. The only one I've heard about on KTVF is "Mr. Music.""

"Right." I turned the gas off to the stove and removed the eggs from the pan, sliding them onto a plate.

Taking the plate from my hands, he asked. "You? *Mister Music?*"

"Yeah, it sounded perfect. I'll play the record from a sound booth for the Romper Room TV program. Gary said to come to the basement of the Northward Building and that I'll mostly do bookkeeping. It's great since no one knows who the master is behind the tunes. I'll feel like I'm reaching out to kids, but from behind the shield of a TV screen. It's an afternoon program, so I'll be here when you get off work." I figured it suited our marriage well.

"Mmm, these eggs are good." He moved the fork to his mouth with increasing speed, bite after bite. "Mr. Music," he mumbled with his mouth full of eggs. "Guess I'll tune into how it goes later." He placed his empty plate by the sink and grabbed his mug. "Bye." He gave me a quick kiss, and out he went to tackle his day as an elementary school teacher.

Huh, did he approve? I looked around at the kitchen tasks ahead of me before I'd leave for my interview. I let out a sigh and shuffled to the couch with a full cup of coffee in hand. On the end table, a postcard was propped against the lamp. I picked it up and reread the back of the card that'd arrived the day before.

Dear Sharon,

You're missed. Looking forward to seeing you at Christmas. Thanks for the postcard of your trip up the ALCAN. Daddy sends his love.

Love, Mom.

WHILE JAMES AND I TRAVELED THE EXPANSE BETWEEN Ohio and Alaska, we'd had no communication with my parents. Not until we arrived. Even then, we'd only jotted notes on postcards and sent them south. A few months had passed since then, and now a return card had arrived.

Christmas in Ohio was out of the question. What did she expect from us? Had she looked at a map to see how far away we were? I put the card back where I'd propped it the day before. Sandwiched between the expectations of parents and a husband, I felt pulled taut on so many levels. Even the weight of the work pulled at me. I tucked my knees under myself and grabbed a blanket from the corner of the couch. Maybe a nap would soften the blows of the not-so-subtle expectations rapidly firing at me.

What would it take to drive me forward and finally find rest? Did I need to work harder? Were there things I wasn't doing right? I closed my eyes and pulled the blanket in close to my face. The soft flannel against my cheek drew me to cuddle up even tighter on the cushion of the couch and rest.

CHAPTER 8

I WASN'T PREPARED FOR THE WINTER OF THE northern boreal forest to begin in late September. The winds of change blew in with termination dust on the Alaska mountain Range to the south. I'd first heard the Alaskan term for the first dusting of snow from James after one of his students had explained it to him. What a horrible image: the termination of summer. Anne Shirley would have had a much more poetic way of describing the first snowfall of the year.

After the light snow in September, some warm days followed, and the snow melted. However, by mid-October, there was a permanent blanket on the grass and the sidewalks were less manageable during walks. Instead, we took Sunday afternoon drives north of town and quickly discovered the taiga was true to the characteristics described in the encyclopedia James had brought home from school.

"Cold biome," I stated out loud as I jotted a descriptive note in a letter I was sending Mary. She'd been in my thoughts throughout this week of December. I looked over at James, who sat grading schoolwork in his chair in the living room. "What else should I tell her?"

"What?" He peeked up from his work and put his pen in his mouth.

"Never mind. I assumed you were listening to me." I was terse with him again, instead of patient. He didn't seem to always track the tension I perceived. Oh, I wanted to show him a devoted love, but I wasn't sure I knew how.

He set his work on his lap and looked at me on the couch. "Go ahead."

I smiled as I spoke to him. "I'm writing Mary a letter and trying to describe to her what I see, feel, and hear. It's hard to portray something with words instead of pictures."

"Oh, I love words." James' smile broadened across his jaw.

Of course he did. "All right then, go ahead, fire away." I held my pen, ready to capture his ideas on paper.

"Intriguing, historical, iconic, and fascinating. Alaska is a treasure worth pursuing with passion." At the word passion, he raised his eyebrows, then gave me a wink. "This friendly state boasts golden opportunity. How's that?"

I wasn't sure I shared his enthusiasm. My interest was growing, but it still had plenty of room for more.

"Hey, speaking of passion, make sure you don't take an extra shift at the TV station this weekend. I have plans." He leaned forward, placing his workload of school papers on the coffee table.

I set my letter on the table next to his pile. "What's up?"

"It's our anniversary next week. We should celebrate every day this month." He sprang to his feet and whisked me off the couch, enveloping me in his arms. He swung me around the room, and I clung to his neck.

"I know it's our anniversary, and I want to celebrate. I just can't think of where to go or what to do."

He stopped spinning and set me down, then drew me close.

"I tell you what, every odd-year anniversary, I'll plan the party, and every even year, you plan. I have everything set up already. This year's mystery location will be revealed by *moi*." He pointed to himself and tapped his chest with his finger.

My gaze fell to my feet. How had a year gone by so fast? Had our love grown, or was it stagnant? I'd promised to follow him to the world's edge, and here we were, moving forward with forever one inch at a time. "James?"

His grip on me lessened, and he stroked my cheek with his palm. "Yes, sweets?"

"I love you."

"Aw, I love you too." He gave me a tender peck on the cheek and stepped over to his chair.

I loved him and our life, but I knew we had room for more. I could do more.

I heard a noise outside and walked to the window to see what the commotion was about. Kids were sledding down the snow berms accumulating in the corners of the front parking lot. The laughter and chaos of children fighting over toboggans told me they were enjoying the winter season.

"Oh, and find some dice, will you? For our date this weekend." James didn't even look up from his work.

I wouldn't let it faze me this time. Dice, dancing, decisions, and I'm sure some deliberation would be the theme of our anniversary.

JAMES POURED ME A GLASS OF SPARKLING CIDER AND then filled his own. He'd been the perfect gentlemen, wooing me like he had on our first date. It warmed me on this bitterly cold evening. The sparkle in the air as we'd walked to the car was unlike anything I'd seen before. How would I tell Mary about it? *The ice in the fog glistened with a spectacular twinkle.* There was beauty in the frozen north.

"Here's to us, sweets. You and me." James and I clinked the goblets and cheered ourselves.

I beamed at my man. "Yes, to us."

"Now, on to business." He cleared his throat and tucked his napkin into the collar of his shirt.

The warmth of the evening was fading, and I pulled my sweater off the back of my chair, avoiding James' gaze and scanning the room of the Switzerland hotel and restaurant. A couple close by swooned over their dinner. Young lovers, I was sure. Another couple sat holding hands, sipping their hot drinks. I assumed they had been married for decades and their well-aged love could rest in silence.

"Do you have the dice?" James held out his hand to me.

The stupid die. Yes, I did. I'd hoped he'd forgotten. Wasn't there a more mature way to spice up the night?

I removed the die from my purse, trying to keep a straight face and not play into his schemes, whatever they may be this time.

"I've been noticing the sad look in your eyes." He tossed the die in one hand. "And I have a proposal. Don't worry, it doesn't involve moving."

I drew in a deep breath. Oh, glory, what now?

James' eyes held a mysterious twinkle, and he reached for my hands, enveloping them with his. "Here, you'll do the deal. I say we let the roll of the dice decide whether on our anniversary we have you…" He paused to clear his throat again. Was he nervous? "Here it is. If you roll a one, we wait one month; two is two months, and so forth. A six, however, means you stop."

I searched his face, unsure of what he implied or suggested. "Stop what?"

He leaned in closer and looked from side to side as though he held a secret he didn't want someone else to overhear. "Stop taking the pill you swallow every morning with your coffee."

Chapter 8

I leaned forward in my chair and mouthed the words to him. *The pill?*

He nodded and did so with a little too much excitement. Was it time to consider having a family?

I brushed the cloth napkin on my lap. "So, just so I understand, every number represents a month, but six means stop?"

"Yup, you've got it," he said and folded his hands in front of him. His carefree ways were ingrained in his everyday mannerisms.

I both loved and struggled with the quality. However, he was ignited with the plan because he was thinking of me.

It didn't sound too bad. Only a one out of a six chance at not taking my morning medication that prevented me from getting pregnant. I felt like chance was on my side with this one. How could I lose?

"I just wondered if a baby would help brighten your eyes," he clarified. "You love kids and are so good with them. I figure we either wait a few months or go for it, but let fate do its magic again and tell us what to do."

It worked for me. I'd decided long ago that I should trust one day as little as possible. Chance ruled the universe. "Sure, I'll roll."

I fumbled with the die in my palm and blew a breath over my hand, then gazed into James' eyes. He'd get to play his game, and I'd have time to mull it over for a few months, at least. I didn't think it was an insensitive suggestion. He was only trying to help. Honestly, the idea of a baby sounded promising, but challenging too. I tossed the die onto the glass table and put a palm over my mouth at the number facing up.

Oh, mercy. Wasn't I the lucky one? *Not another six!*

"Oh, baby, baby!" James chimed. He jumped up from his chair and held out his hand.

I moved with him to the middle of the room.

"Can I have this dance?" he asked quietly. "I can't imagine life without you, sweets. I'm not always the most sensitive guy, but I sure am lucky I've got you."

"Love you too, James," I replied and swayed with him to the music and let the question linger in my mind of how long it might take to get pregnant? Certainly, it'd be months of trying, giving us time to prepare.

CHAPTER 9

THE HOLIDAYS CAME AND WENT, AND WE CELEBRATED New Year's with some of the other teachers from the school. January ushered in some cold weather, and we soon went back to our usual routine with James at school and me at the radio station.

On this February day, things were anything but routine. I retched at the aroma of the coffee I smelled from where I lay in our room. I shakily propped myself up on my elbow and looked at the clock, squinting my eyes. Good grief, it was already ten in the morning. How had I slept in so late? Falling back to my pillow, I placed a hand on my clammy forehead and groaned. The bathroom seemed so far away, but I knew as soon as I sat up, I'd need to barrel myself to it like stampeding cattle toward the range.

James' ears must have been fine-tuned to hear me inch out bed because he appeared in the doorway with a pained look on his face. He came over to me with a towel in his hand. "If I'd known you'd be so sick, I would never have suggested we try to have a baby."

"If I had known we'd get pregnant in a matter of weeks, I

would have chanted over the dice a few more times, pleading for better luck."

At the last word, I gulped and got out of bed. My dry throat was drawing a wave of nausea from deep inside me, and I pushed past James to the hallway.

After wiping my face in the bathroom, I inched to the living room and curled up on the couch. "Can you get me some ice-cold water?" I spoke to James with my eyes shut.

"Anything, sweets."

James' care for my every need had been phenomenal. I felt so guilty, lying in bed for days on end. It was already the end of February and the monotonous, overwhelming nausea seemed as though it would never resolve.

He brought a cup to me and placed in on the coffee table, then placed a rag to my forehead. "Sharon, I know you'll make an amazing mom. The doctor said it will pass soon, then it will be smooth sailing to the end."

I wanted to rip the rag from his hands and toss him across the room. *Smooth sailing to the end?* Where was his head? The end meant agonizing birthing pains. I may never do this again.

I mouthed the word *water*.

"There you go. Small sips. Good girl." He placed a hand on my shoulder, and I came unglued.

"Good girl!" I paused and took a drink, letting the water slide down my dry throat. "James, be quiet!"

I didn't like my brisk response to James' attempts at comforting me, but I presumed most women who were expecting had some element of disdain during their pregnancy. It had to be normal. There also had to be a relief from the torment of a raw throat caused by incessant puking.

James didn't show any emotion at my comment, and he stayed at my side in spite of it. His lingering spoke of love and care. Guilt settled in, and I closed my eyes to focus on the positives of the moment. I had a husband who tended to me. He was helping and reaching out and trying to encourage me. Would I have the patience to parent, which was surely more trying than early pregnancy?

I let the whisper out from my parched lips. "I'm sorry."

James cupped my face with his hands. "It's okay. I love you. I'll try not to say dumb things."

I almost let out a laugh. He didn't mean to be insensitive. He just couldn't imagine what it was like for me.

He let go of my face and walked back over to the kitchen. "Maybe you should call your mom again and ask her for advice. She birthed you and your brother, and I'm sure there are things she learned along the way."

Thankfully, James was busy in the kitchen and didn't notice me roll my eyes at the mention of my mom. Call her? I'd only called to inform my parents about the news of our pregnancy. I wasn't only trying to avoid criticism, I also wasn't keen on getting their advice.

Somehow, I wanted to parent differently than I'd been raised. I didn't have the answers, but I was determined to find the right techniques and have a list to follow. As soon as I felt better, there would be books to pore over and magazine articles to hunt down with rigor. The job at the TV station would provide ample time to read about and study pregnancy and motherhood. Surely, with enough information, I wouldn't fall short.

I'm certain my raging hormones were to blame for the shift in my focus, but I was dwelling on the inward pounding of my heart and my desires, with no room for anything else at the moment. I laid my head back.

James moved into the living room. I could hear his humming. He tapped on the coffee table, then spoke in a hushed tone. "If you'll be okay for about an hour, I have an errand to run."

"Um-hm." It felt exacerbating to respond. I yielded to the demand of rest.

A WOMAN'S VOICE?

My nonsense dreams flitted away like a chickadee off to a new tree. I'd heard someone talking, and a familiar ring of laughter filled the room. I willed myself to wake up and find out who was there. It felt like I was prying open my eyelids with a crowbar. *Why couldn't I wake up?* I shifted my legs and stretched my toes. If I twitched and turned, maybe my body would respond and I could be part of the world that was going on without me.

"Shh, we woke her up. Darn it. She must be so tired." It was Mary's voice carrying over the hum of the heater.

"Mary?" I spoke with only a morsel of strength and barely opened my eyes to see my sister-in-law tiptoe toward me.

Her smile spread across her face as she came to my side and kneeled down next to me. "My sweet, sugar-and-spice." Her warm hands touched my cheeks. "Oh, you poor thing! I'm here. Close your eyes and go back to the dreamworld. Dream of your baby, and I'll visit you later." She rubbed my forehead and gently placed her fingers on my eyelids, shutting them. "Ssh..."

I let the balm of her touch and kind words soothe my body and mind. Could I drift back into the land of dreams where I held my swaddled baby, knowing the worst was over and we could enjoy him and go on with a happy life as a family?

CHAPTER 10

JAMES SAT IN HIS USUAL SPOT IN THE LIVING ROOM while Mary and I doodled at the kitchen table. I'd surfaced from my morning sickness after a few days of bed rest and could now appreciate Mary's surprise visit to Alaska.

"I love coloring." Mary grabbed a new crayon from the center of the table where the crayons sat in a mason jar. "It takes the aches and pains of the day and colors them in the brightest pinks and purples. I can take on the world with a fresh perspective."

Her crayon broke as she spoke, and we both laughed at her vigor.

"Huh, I guess even coloring has its trials," she said.

I placed a hand softly on my belly. Soon there would be movement inside, but for now, my bloated stomach was a reminder to proceed with caution so the nausea wouldn't resurface. "I'm so glad you came." I beamed at Mary and hoped she saw the genuine, warm feelings I had for her.

"My pleasure. I'll admit that I was afraid of flying here in the dead of winter, but I was pleasantly surprised when I arrived. Beauty surrounds you here. The glitter of snow reminds me of diamonds. There is a raw purity in the undisturbed white fluff on the hills." She picked up a crayon and studied it with her eyes. "And then, my sugar, there is you. I would have traveled the world to be close to you and help coddle you while you're incubating."

My nose scrunched, and I searched her face. "Incubating? Good grief, Mary, I'm not a chicken. I feel like a train engine has railroaded me at full speed, but I don't plan on sitting on my rump my whole pregnancy."

Mary exchanged her crayons with ones from the jar. "I'm just playing, Sharon. Maybe today we can go out for a walk. Some fresh air will do you good."

James came over from the living room and leaned in toward me. "It's so great to have you up and feeling better, sweets." He placed a kiss on the top of my head. "I'm headed over to the school to get some things ready for Monday. Call my room if you need anything."

"Don't worry about us. I'll take good care of her!" Mary stood and walked to the stove. "I'll get some tea brewing."

I looked up at James. "Thank you again for helping Mary come visit." His efforts to show me love were clear in his thoughtfulness. I'd need to remember to always be grateful for this quality in him.

"My pleasure." He moved to the entryway, bundled up, and called out, "Bye, ladies."

I shifted in my chair, then stood up, bracing myself on the table. "Maybe if I feel up to it, I can show you the TV station. I have an entire wall of pictures kids have sent to Mr. Music. You'll get a kick out of them."

Sharon came over with the teapot and set it on the table. "And there you go, always including the kids. You're going to be an amazing mom."

One could only hope she was right. But were there any guar-

Chapter 10

antees in life? I had deep-seated flaws I hoped to overcome with knowledge. "Thanks, Mary. So, how long are you staying? I'm sure you told me, but this whole past week is a blur." I poured myself a cup of tea and took an initial, careful sip of the gingery blend.

"Sugar?" She held the bowl out to me, and I spooned some into my teacup. "I booked a one-way ticket here."

"Mary!"

Joy bubbled inside me, and I wanted to jump up and hug her. Instead, a broad smile stretched across my face, and I reached for her hand and squeezed it. Then I took another sip of my tea, feeling its warmth and the herbs sooth my stomach.

"I'm here as long as you need me," she said, before sipping her own tea.

Oh, did I ever need her friendship and support. There were so many things I wanted to share with her. Longings stirred within me—longings I'd hidden deep down and away from James. I was up for a grand Alaskan adventure, but my sense of self and who I was in all of it weren't yet crisp and clear in my mind. Would she be able to help me? Maybe this pregnancy was a gift to help me find my grand purpose. Yes, there were questions swirling like the wind when it captures the snow in a drift, holding its force in place until it builds into a heap.

"Look." Mary quickened her steps as she moved to the window. "Earlier this morning, the tiniest little flakes were falling, but now they're huge!"

I wrapped my arms around my waist and came to where she was, next to the window. Outside, the scene looked like a snow globe, flakes falling in a mad dash to cover the sidewalks and cars. "I love the snow here. Some of our friends invited us to cross-country ski by the university and it was a riot. I fell all over the place. Hey, I know"—I turned to face Mary, who stood, wide-eyed, watching the blizzard—"we could take you on a drive to see Mount McKinley! We've been wanting to do the trip since spring."

"Sounds good to me. Are you feeling well enough for a walk? Or do you want to let the tea settle in your belly first?" Mary's look of concern comforted me.

"I think a walk would be great. I'll go get changed."

I eased into my room and found some warm clothes. The culture here placed little emphasis on style and decorative clothing. Necessity and warmth triumphed. I was glad for the items I'd found at Army and Navy store. They weren't the prettiest things, but they made being out in the elements tolerable. I was slipping on some wool socks when I heard James' voice in the hall.

"Sharon!" His voice held panic and intensity. "Sharon!"

"What is it?" I called out. I made my way to the door and almost ran into him.

"There's been an accident. Gary flagged me down and asked us to come and help. Grab your coat. Hurry." He spoke without looking at me and yelled for Mary to grab warm clothes for herself, just in case.

"James." I placed my hand on his shoulder and tried to catch his gaze. "What's going on?"

"There's no time to talk. We have to go, now!" He tugged at my arm, and I followed him to where Mary stood by the door. We all hurried out in silence.

ALL OF JAMES' FOCUS WAS ON DRIVING, AND HE didn't say a word until we pulled into the Piggly Wiggly supermarket. He turned off the engine. "Let me go see what's going on, and I'll be right back."

James rushed to the group gathering in front of the store, where people stood with shovels and long ski poles.

Chapter 10

"I wonder what's going on?" I said, as I squinted my eyes to make sense of the chaos of the crowd amidst the snowstorm.

A stranger walked to the car and tapped on the window. I opened my door.

"Hey, can you ladies help too? There are some kids trapped under a pile of snow that broke loose off the roof while they were passing by. We could use you inside with supplies."

"Of course." Mary and I spoke in unison.

We got out of the car and walked past James. I tapped his shoulder. "We'll be inside."

He nodded at me, obviously engrossed in the instructions someone was giving the group.

We entered the store. Loud voices filled the building as panic escalated. Mary put her arm through mine and drew me to the middle of the group where a woman was trying to get everyone's attention. My neck tingled as all my senses jetted toward high alert out of concern for the trapped children.

"If you could all be quiet!" The older lady raised her voice above the crowd. "I need one group to pull blankets off the shelves and another one to make hot drinks. Then some of you can clear out a space here." She waved her arms close to the entrance. "Clear the area and set up some chairs close together so we can huddle in close when the kids come in from the cold."

Come in? She assumed they'd be okay? Thank God.

"I'll help make the drinks," I said, and the lady nodded.

Together, Mary and I found our way to the side of the building where there were employees opening containers of hot chocolate. We worked in silence, gathering supplies and moving them close to the circle of chairs.

Minutes seemed like hours. Everyone eventually completed their tasks, then we sat on the chairs with our fingers crossed, waiting to hear news of recovery. Finally, a strong gust of wind from the open door was followed by snow-covered children, who came in rubbing their faces and brushing the snow from their coats.

Mary and I gave up our seats and worked to bring the kids warm drinks to melt the icicles of panic from their core. My nausea subsided as I served others.

At one point, I knelt beside a young girl about five or six, warming her toes with my hands. Her shy smile was the only thanks I needed. Maybe I'd have a sweet girl like her? Her dark hair hung over her face, and she brushed it aside.

"Your mom will be here soon." I spoke quietly and reassuringly.

"I hope my mommy isn't mad at me," the girl said before coughing.

"Oh, no, she won't be mad. She will so happy you're okay."

She coughed some more, then spoke so softly that I had to lean closer to hear.

"Uh, I don't know. We were supposed to wait for a teacher before we walked that way. My mom's usually upset when I don't obey."

I didn't know how to answer her. Wouldn't any parent be glad their child was safe? "If you were my little girl, I'd give you a big hug. How about when you see your mom, you hug her tight?"

The girl's face lit up, and she smiled as she drew her cup to her mouth for a sip of hot cocoa.

I removed my hands from her feet and stood up. "I have a little secret. It might help you warm you up. Do you ever listen to Mr. Music?"

Her eyes widened, and she nodded.

"I'm Mr. Music. I go to the TV station and play the music. Except I'm not a mister, I'm a missus." I wondered if she understood as she scrunched her eyebrows.

"Wow," was all she said as she looked at me from the top of my head to my toes.

Chapter 10

I heard James laughing behind me, and I turned to watch him walk closer. "There you are. About ready to go? Looks like they have things covered here now."

I nodded to James, then kneeled down near my new, little friend. "I'm going now. Remember, Mrs. Music says hug your momma real tight."

In the cutest small voice, she answered, "I will."

As we drove back to the apartment, I couldn't push the face of the little girl out of my mind. An avalanche of snow from a nearby roof had almost buried a small group of children. Perhaps it was the influx of hormones raging within my body, but I shook, even though my body was warm.

How did parents part with their kids even for a second when something could happen to them so unexpectedly? My teeth chattered. Why was I coming undone?

"Sharon, are you okay?" James placed his hand on my shoulder.

"I-I-I'm...ok-k-kay," I stammered out the response. But I wasn't okay. In my mind, she was my little girl, and she'd been cold and worried that I would be mad at her.

The snow outside was beautiful, but in large numbers, the snowflakes could accumulate into an avalanche and the unstoppable force would bury you in a heartbeat, just like the doubts and fears multiplying in my heart. Would I have a love for my baby, where I'd care for them at all costs? Already, I was hoping to be the best mom I could be, but I didn't even feel like I matched my own expectations as a wife. "J-James?"

"I'm here. Hold on, we're almost home." James rubbed my shoulder with the assumption I was cold.

"I wa-wa-want to b-be a g-good mom." I crossed my arms around my waist and tried to hold in the emotion of worry welling inside.

"You'll do great," Mary cheered me from the back seat.

"You're probably dehydrated, and it's why you're shaking. Hang on, girl, and we'll get you some tea soon."

James patted my knee. "You already are a wonderful mom, sweets. You already are."

I closed my eyes and saw the face of the sweet girl. I imagined myself hugging her and holding her tight, rescuing her from her worry and reassuring her she was safe and loved.

CHAPTER 11

A MONTH LATER MARKED MY TWELFTH WEEK OF pregnancy, and I was feeling alive again. The bright blue skies and other signs of spring welcomed me on my walks to the TV station.

I sat inside the office and sipped some tea as I neared the end of my workday in the early-afternoon hours, thinking about how life changed as dramatically as the seasons.

Mary reasoned my pregnancy had driven me to introspection, and she didn't make light of the far-off looks I sometimes had when I sat in the living room. She'd even suggested I begin a journal of sorts or take up a new hobby to help me focus my feelings.

I'd found a book of poetry at the library and studied the formats of various poems. Perhaps pouring out my perceptions on paper would be a way to sort and understand my emotions. When Mary went back to Ohio last week, I'd stopped at the drugstore and bought a small notebook to try her idea.

I wrote the octave and sestet pattern for a sonnet, knowing the octave introduced the conflict and the sestet the solution.

Would poetry help me work through the ache burning inside?

I found two words and then jotted down rhymes to coincide with each of them. It would be easy to rhyme my problem: sad.

The phrases came easily, and I finished the octave. I stared at the page. Where would I find the solution to complete the sonnet? A feeling was simple to describe, but I didn't have a prescription for *sad*. Perhaps if I knew what caused me feel that way? Was something missing in my life? I spoke the words out loud to myself.

"My face doesn't hide how I feel: sad.
    Is there an unseen foe?
    I've tilled the soil of my soul to grow.
    There's no claim I've somehow been bad.
    I search for my heart to be glad.
    Is there a way to know?
    For my eternal destiny to show?
    It's not a rhyme I seek, or a fad."

What was I sad about?

Forget it. I shifted the notebook aside and stood up to go to the window.

It was a gorgeous spring day. The sun held enough intensity to melt snow from the roof, and drips of water fell to the ground. Then an idea sprang into my mind. I'd go to James' class and say hi. It was nice weather to walk the several blocks to his school. I picked up my notebook and placed it in my tote.

I stomped the snow from my boots in the entryway of Nordale Elementary and walked the short hall to James' sixth-grade class. Even several steps before the door, I could hear the uproar of the class. What were they up to now? I peered around the doorway and saw all the desks pushed to the side of the

Chapter 11

room and the children sitting on the floor, roaring with laughter. What was so funny?

James sat in the middle of the group and jumped up when he saw me in the doorway. He clapped his hands. "All right, the missus is here. Put the desks back, and get ready for your sustained reading time."

The children groaned in unison, and the sound echoed around the room. James gave me a wink, then moved to his desk, grabbed a paper, and walked back over to me. "Hi, sweets. Will you look it over and tell me your thoughts?"

I took the paper from his hand and scanned it. A letter? Yes, a letter from the school board. He'd need to decide if he would return next year. I reread the brief paragraphs. James pulled a chair close to his desk and patted the seat. I sat down after I removed my coat.

"What's your gut tell you?" I questioned him as I handed it back to him.

James glanced around the room and smiled at the kids shuffling desks and getting settled. "I'll miss it, but we need to be close to family when the baby is born. Yesterday, I called Mary and had her search postings for jobs down there." He looked at me and took my hand. "Unless you think we should stay?"

"When we came, I had no expectations of how long we'd be here. It's been an adventure, but I'm ready to go back." I crossed my legs. "Ugh, except for the long drive."

"Ha, you'll probably sleep most of the way." He gave my hand a squeeze. "There's still two months of school left. We should plan some brief trips while we're here. We never made it to Mount McKinley. And there's Anchorage and Seward. I still have some places I'd like to see before we head south."

"All right. When should I give my notice at the station?"

"Any time, then we can be weekend warriors and do some road trips." He sat straighter in his chair, inching toward the edge of his seat.

I cracked up at his antics. He was always eager for more. He loved seeing the sights and experiencing all that Alaska had to offer.

"Oh, James. You're too much. I'll see you later." I got up and buttoned my coat.

After visiting the kindergarten class to say hi to all the little ones, I left the school and strolled down the street. The spring air was invigorating. Fairbanks would hold special memories for me. I'd miss our life and our routine, but I was ready to see our families and share our little one with them.

I placed my hand on my belly. My bump had appeared a couple of weeks ago. At my most recent appointment, the doctor had made a comment about how big I already was. The sixties were ushering in new ideas about what pregnant women should look like, and they advised me to watch what I ate. I was taken aback. I'd hardly eaten when I was so sick for weeks on end. I assured the physician it was all baby and not an ounce of extra weight.

Earlier, the word that came to mind when I reflected on my feelings was *sad*. Now I felt an inkling of the joy that came with anticipation. Our move back to Ohio, a new baby, and being surrounded by family would certainly brighten my outlook.

I smiled to myself. A new baby. Last year I was working for the Ohio Edison Company and learning how to cook supper for two. Soon, I'd be a stay-at-home mom learning how to sew cloth diapers. If things had changed so drastically after just one year, what would my life look like two years from now? I shook my head. I was racing too far ahead.

CHAPTER 12

I placed my empty teacup and saucer on the coffee table. Mary came from the kitchen of her apartment with a bowl of Jell-o salad and handed it to me. My third trimester was taking its toll, and I put my feet up on the coffee table. Today, I didn't care if it might appear rude; my swollen feet were throbbing. Now, at the first week of October, I had officially reached thirty-six weeks gestation, and each day felt like a year.

"So, what did the doctor say?" Mary took a spoonful of her Jell-o and searched my face.

I chuckled. "He said, 'wow!'"

"And?" She leaned closer to me. "He must have said more than that."

"Oh, yes." I rubbed my massive belly. "He also said, 'that must be one big boy in there!'" I felt the baby thump my ribs, and I massaged my lower abdomen. "I told him, 'I agree, and our little guy must have learned martial arts because he performs karate on my kidneys.'"

Mary's face held a wide smile, and she ate another spoonful of Jell-O. "Did he say how much longer? I know you said you were due in late October, but you look like you could explode any minute, and it's barely the first part of the month."

A familiar cramp in my belly took my shallow breath away, and I clasped the couch cushion, sucking in a quick gasp and holding it.

"Are you okay?" Mary moved closer and knelt beside me.

I closed my eyes and nodded in response. It took everything I had to concentrate on the Braxton Hicks contraction, which eased after half a minute. I pursed my lips and breathed out. "Oh golly, those have been happening twice a day. Um, now... Sorry. What did you say?" I looked at Mary, who held her hand over her mouth.

"Jeepers. You're one tough momma. I saw your belly move with that one. Never mind my prodding. Can I get you anything?" Mary stood up and moved to the kitchen, looking over her shoulder. "Tea? Coffee?"

"How about a time machine to zip me into mid-November after the baby has arrived so I can skip labor."

Mary called out from the kitchen. "Fresh out of those, sis. Relax, I'll make us some more tea. Now, you were telling me about James' job earlier. How's he adjusting to being back?"

I heard Mary busy herself with cups and spoons, which clinked on the counter. The familiar space of her apartment was comforting after our transition year away. I closed my eyes and took in slow breaths. "He likes it and seems to have slid right back into the groove. Our evenings are full of stories about the kids in his class."

A pain seized me, and I cried out before I could control myself. "Ah!" The contraction spread from my back to my front and the intensity was beyond anything I'd felt before. I simultaneously clasped my mouth with one hand and my lower abdomen with the other. I opened my eyes wide, searching for Mary. "Help!"

The shattering in the kitchen pierced my ears. "Sharon!" I could hear Mary call out to me, but I couldn't see her.

What kept her? The pain held me in place, and I couldn't

Chapter 12

move. I tried to breathe properly, but I couldn't even remember if I was supposed to pant, inhale deeply, or what. Weren't those birthing classes we'd attended supposed to stick with me when the contractions squeezed the life out of you? The room spun, and I closed my eyes.

"I'm here, Sharon. Hold on. I need to call James." Her touch on my arm reinforced her presence, and then I heard her scurry away, followed by her muffled words in the distance.

As the pain loosened its grip, my mind flooded with questions. Was it too soon to have the baby? I'd not packed a bag for the hospital yet. Didn't the doctor say there was more to check before the baby arrived? I felt like I was floating in a rolling river with no control of where I would land.

A powerful, rhythmic kick in my belly reminded me that the life inside me demanded my wholehearted attention. James and I had nicknamed our child, who we assumed would be a son: Nugget. We figured he was our lucky little guy, rising from the depths of destiny, and he'd forge his path no matter where he was, or what lie ahead of him. He was diligently active and loved putting on a show. James would give me a play-by-play of the belly movements he could see when I lay still at night. He figured Nugget already enjoyed football.

"Hang in there, Nugget," I whispered. "Can you hold on a little longer?"

I opened my eyes and saw Mary pacing in the kitchen next to where I sat. She placed the phone on its receiver, then came over to me. "We've got a plan. There will be no arguing about it." She pointed her finger at me as though she were scolding a young child. "Just stay where you are, and your brother will be here soon to take us to the hospital. He was the only one I could get through to." Mary wrung her hands and then stopped. "I'm sorry." She knelt beside me. "I should be the strong one here."

I touched Mary's hand. "Thanks, sis." As I finished my sentence, another contraction railed me, and I squeezed Mary's hand with all my strength. I combed my mind for the birthing mantra I'd memorized, which somehow had escaped any working memory I had.

"I...hope...this...wave...ends...soon." Mary squeezed out her words.

Wave! That was it! *Each wave brings me closer to my baby!*

The contraction waned, and I eased my grip on Mary.

"Oh my word! Sharon." Mary jumped up and down, then ran over to the sink and turned on the water, shaking her hand under the steady stream.

I licked my parched lips and let out a deep sigh. "James is missing out. Where'd you say he is?"

"I didn't say. I couldn't get ahold of him. He's missing out all right. There won't be any fingers left on my hand if you keep that up."

Standing up, I smoothed my polyester shirt. "Phew, I've got to go to the bathroom." I shuffled down the hall. "Each wave, each wave, each wave," I repeated to myself.

"What?" Mary called out from the kitchen.

"Just saying each wave—" As I stepped from the hall into the bathroom, a trickle flowed down my leg. "Mary! My water!"

Mary's steps sounded more like an elephant charging as her tiny frame ran down the hall to me. "Wave? Water?"

A puddle was forming at my feet. "Each wave"—I picked up my foot and moved it over from the puddle—"brings me closer to my baby." I held my hand over my chest and fixed my gaze on Mary. "I've got to get it together because our baby is running for a touchdown." My heart pounded. All I wanted was for James to carry me in his powerful arms and tell me everything was going to be okay.

Chapter 12

THE SMELL OF THE MEDICINAL LOTION THE NURSE had rubbed on my back tickled my nose. Its cooling effect had temporarily relieved the cramp in my lower back and also sent tingles down my tailbone. My resolve for the end of this trial was to be the happiest woman alive. It was the chance of a lifetime to love my son with a purity and selflessness. There would be so much to celebrate. I squirmed my feet under the crisp sheets. Over the last few weeks, as part of my birthing preparation, I'd promised myself I'd bounce back after the birth and be ready to face my mothering adventure.

James and I had spent the last few evenings eating popcorn and reading books out loud to our Nugget. One evening in particular, James had talked about raising an entire football team. Grateful for his love of children, I'd pasted on a smile, but under the layers of pretense, I wasn't so sure about those numbers.

The nurse situated her supplies on the bed next to me. "All right hun, I'm going to need you to lie still while I check your baby's heartbeat." The fluttering kicks had decreased over the last hour that I'd been at the hospital, and I was curious to know what she'd find. Was I progressing? Would things move quickly now that my water had broken?

I focused on my breathing while I watched the nurse's face. I assumed she was an experienced RN because her gray hair was pinned back under her starched white hat. She also moved with methodical grace in the birthing room and had only spoken with gentleness and care since I'd arrived.

Her blue eyes smiled at me, and then she raised her eyebrows. "Huh." She set down her listening tool and folded her hands. "All right, I'm going to palpate your abdomen so I can get a better understanding of the position of the baby. I might be capturing your heart rate, which is making it hard to hear baby's. I'll go wash my hands so they are nice and warm before I touch your belly." She moved to the sink, and when she turned her back, I placed my hand on my stomach.

I was certain the baby was head down and kicking my diaphragm, and yet I felt elbows and knees down lower as well. I didn't know. I'd lost track over the last couple of weeks, trying to ignore the movement so I could sleep, yet I felt so happy to feel the life inside me.

When the nurse returned, she positioned her hand on my belly and tilted her head to one side, then looked up into the corner of the room. I watched her closely for clues of what she might be sensing. Her eyes shifted to me, and she gave me a wide smile. "Your little guy is going to be here soon, my dear. I'll listen again, now that I've discovered his hiding place."

Hiding place! Good grief, he was protruding out two feet in front of me.

She placed her metallic tool on the side of my abdomen for a couple of minutes. "What's that called?" I asked as she removed it.

"It's called a Pinard. I'll need to listen one more time, dear." She walked to the other side of the bed and placed the Pinard on my other side. "Ah ha! As I gathered." She placed her tool on the bed and touched my shoulder. "I'll go tell the doctor and be right back. When he comes in, I'll go see if your husband has made it to the waiting room."

"Oh, yes. Thanks." I wanted to see James' face and feel his touch. He never would have guessed his school day would mean a field trip to the hospital. Why couldn't the school get ahold of him? Thankfully, my brother had left Mary with me, then went looking for James. What would we have done without family nearby?

I let out a sigh and then took in as deep a breath as I could with my son pushing inside me like he was kicking me out of my own body.

Since my water broke, the contractions had lessened and

were manageable. I wiggled my toes and looked around the sterile room. I heard many mumbling voices, which carried into the room from the hallway. I lay still, curious as to whether I could make out what was being said. Nope, they'd built the walls too thick. I'm sure they didn't want women to hear other mothers crying out with birthing pangs.

There was still a mountain to climb with this labor. I whispered, "But each wave brings me closer to my son." After placing my hand on my belly, I stroked it. "I love you, little Nugget. I mean big Nugget!"

Would he have James' dark features and hair? Or my bright blue eyes? Maybe a combination of both of us. I'd had many dreams of holding him in my arms and promising him I'd watch over him and keep him safe.

"Shh," someone said as the door to my room opened. Four people walked in. Two were nurses, including the one who'd admitted me. One was my doctor, Dr. Herbert, and I assumed the man next to him was also a doctor since he wore a white lab coat and had a stethoscope around his neck.

"Mrs. Kline, how nice to see you again so soon." Dr. Hebert walked to the right side of my bed and shook my hand. "I'd like to introduce an intern. His name is Mr. Pale." Dr. Herbert smiled. "Hopefully, he doesn't go pale when we deliver." Dr. Hebert laughed at his own joke and then gestured to the intern with an outstretched hand.

"Nice to meet you, Mr. Pale," I said to the intern, who held a pad of paper and a pen and fumbled them as he moved to shake my hand.

"Yes, ma'am." He nodded to me, then jotted on his paper.

Dr. Hebert moved closer to the head of the bed. "Ahem. Mrs. Kline, I was hoping your husband would be here when we had to do this, but we have to move forward."

Do what? "Is everything okay?" I asked, clasping my hands on my belly.

"Nurse Kelly came across some interesting findings in the examination she gave you when you were admitted, and I'm going to assess you myself. I have the utmost confidence in her thirty years as a nurse. She was practically born with a Pinard in her hand. She's the baby expert here."

I noted the smiles shared between the nurse and the doctor. They seemed jovial. What could the news be?

"Now, Mr. Pale," Dr. Herbert continued, "you'll need to set your pad of paper down and touch the patient. Determine where you should place your stethoscope and begin when you're ready. I'll auscultate on this side."

Mr. Pale set his notepad on a counter behind him and then put the stethoscope in his ears and placed it on me. I watched each of their faces as eyebrows rose up on Mr. Pale's face and then the doctors.

A contraction began, and I grabbed at the sheets as the intensity increased. I closed my eyes and breathed through the pangs, remembering the plan Nurse Kelly and I had gone over to take nice, slow breaths.

Someone touched my shoulder and rubbed it. I almost spoke out for them to stop. When the pain subsided, I opened my eyes and saw James next to me with wide eyes and a huge grin on his face.

"Sweets!" He leaned over me and gave me a kiss on top of my head. "I'm so sorry. I didn't know the baby could come so early. You know I would have taken time off had I known. I left the kids with—"

He quieted and held my hand. "Uh, I'll stop talking now. How's it going, doctor? Is she okay?"

"You're just in time, Mr. Kline. My intern and I were just listening to the healthy heartbeats of your babies." The doctor put his stethoscope around his neck and smiled.

"Babies? But we have just one in there," I said and shifted myself in bed to sit up straight.

Nurse Kelly came over next to James and put her arm around his shoulder. "My dears, you are the proud parents of not one, but two babies," she said.

I saw James buckle. Perhaps it's why the nurse held onto him—she knew the effect it would have. I searched James' broad eyes, which stared at my own.

"Honey?" I said. "We might just have the team you talked about."

"Twins? You said twins? There's two?" James' brow beaded with sweat.

Dr. Hebert pulled a pen out of his lab coat pocket. "I'll move your gown over to the side a minute." He proceeded to draw on my belly. He wrote the numeral one and then handed the pen to Mr. Pale. "Draw a two, Mr. Pale."

Mr. Pale was drawing on my belly when another contraction took my body by force, and I grabbed at the handrails.

Through pursed lips I stammered, "How are…we going to… manage…TWO?" The pain increased, and the noise faded from my ears. I felt dizzy and nauseated. Did I have the resolve to birth not one, but two babies? James was here, but he wasn't telling me everything was going to be okay. A heat wave overcame me in my lightheadedness. I wished someone would reassure me. I suddenly felt numb.

Would it be okay?

CHAPTER 13

James held Roberta in his arms while I cuddled Brooke. Our girls were safely here after a few hours of labor. It didn't seem possible that that morning I'd awakened and talked to my baby boy, Nugget, and now I held one of my *two* daughters swaddled in a pink flannel blanket. What were the chances, back in the frigid month of January, that we'd not only conceive, but conceive twins?

"Remember the first time we saw the northern lights?" I asked James.

"Yes," he said as he gently rocked Roberta. "It was the evening of our anniversary, and we walked and walked out in the cold, mesmerized by the dancing green and purple streams in the sky."

As James held our youngest daughter, I beamed at him and how he watched her with a tender look.

"I remember how awestruck I was at the colors and how surprised I was that we could hear them crackle," I said, thinking about the static electricity that lit the sky that night. "That was the most magical experience I'd ever had until today. Can you believe it?"

Chapter 13

"Can hardly deny it, sweets. Here they are. And she has your brother's blue eyes," James said, holding his gaze on Roberta.

"What?" I asked.

Brooke squirmed in my arms and began a series of hiccups.

"Your brother." James glanced up at me. "He has blue eyes." He paused. "Whereas my entire family has dark eyes." He attempted to clarify his statement.

I searched his face and raised my eyebrows as I spoke. "James." I purposely softened my voice. "*I* have blue eyes."

He moved from where he sat at the foot of the bed closer to where I was. He stared at me and opened his eyes wide, his gaze darting back and forth between my one eye and my other. "That's a gas! You *do* have blue eyes! And they're the most beautiful eyes I've ever seen." He reached over and gave me a peck on the cheek.

I shook my head. My James. What a hoot. "*You're* a gas! I can't believe you didn't know what color eyes I have. And just so you know, all babies have blue eyes when they're born."

James held Roberta out to me, and we switched babies. "How did the doctors miss *this*!" He lifted Brooke up in the air.

"The nurse explained it was the position of the babies. It doesn't matter now." I unwrapped Roberta's blanket and looked at her tiny hands sticking out of her pale-green gown. "They're perfect."

The love pulsating through me for my girls was unlike anything I'd ever experienced. I stroked Brooke's cheek with my fingertip, and she wrinkled her nose at my touch. Now, as they lay peacefully sleeping, I wondered, Could there ever be anything purer than a newborn baby? Their life was a blank slate laid out before them, untouched. What impression would I mark on it?

"Your mom said she'd be by first thing in the morning and so would Mary."

My mom. Why did my stomach turn in a knot at the mention of her? "Mmm," I answered, not looking up.

"Oh, gosh. We're going to need more of everything! I'm going to have to go shopping." James laid Brooke down on the bed. "I don't shop in the baby section. How will I know what these wrinkly babies need?"

I chuckled at James' antics and the brief panic breaking out across his face and creased eyebrows. "Wrinkly babies?" I questioned.

"Yeah, look at them! All wrinkled up and…" His face turned from quizzical to a smile, and then he flattened his lips. "I'm sorry. But now—oh wow! Why hadn't I thought of all the…I've got double duty to be ready for. We're going to need twice the money and…"

I placed my arm on his knee. "James." Would my touch calm his bunny trail of emotion?

"I know!" He lifted his arm in the air, holding up his pointer finger. "We'll take up your mom's offer to come to the house each day and help."

Help from my mom? Averting my eyes, I rewrapped Roberta, swaddling her tight and drawing her close. I felt the warmth of her against my chest and drew in her scent. I supposed my mom had had similar feelings for me when I was born. What had come between us? Why did we hold each other at arm's length? I'd only ever tried to please her. To show her I loved her with my obedience.

James picked up Brooke and hummed to himself as he walked next to the bed.

"James?" I asked, wanting him to help resolve the feelings that were surfacing now that the pain of the birthing was not forefront in my mind.

"Yes, sweets," he answered and intently watched my face.

I wiggled my toes and repositioned myself under the sheets. "Do you think we'll be good parents?"

He stopped, tilted his head, and looked out the window. Did he question himself too?

"By golly, I have no clue what I'm doing," he answered and resumed pacing back and forth next to the bed, humming again.

Did we have a chance at showing our girls a true-felt love? Did we have what it took to provide for them physically and emotionally? The expected baby boy was a challenge I'd mustered up the courage to face. Two baby girls meant needing more than an ocean of reserve to draw from. Where would I find help?

There would have to be information I could digest somewhere.

Roberta fussed, and I stroked her head. Her fine, soft hair had patches still matted to her scalp. I repositioned her and rubbed her back and a faint whimper pricked my ears.

We'd do our best. For my part, these girls would know I'd be there for them and love them and that I'd be the best mom I could.

EARLY THE NEXT MORNING, I MADE AN ATTEMPT TO feed the girls before the nurse ushered the babies back to the nursery. After they were gone, I felt my stomach, where the girls had nestled for nine months, and sat in awe of the fact that they'd arrived.

I sipped my tea and looked out the window, watching the leaves blowing from the trees. Their colors made the passage into fall as obvious as the journey into motherhood that lay before me. There was much to learn and juggle, including how to share the girls with the rest of the family.

"Hello?" a voice called out, and the door to my room opened.

My mom walked in, holding a giftwrapped box in one arm

and a bouquet of flowers in the opposite hand. Her eyes softened when she saw me.

"Hi, Mom," I said as I straightened myself in my bed and set down my cup. "The nurse just took the girls to the nursery. Do you want me to call her back?"

She looked around the room, set the box down on the bed, and came to me with open arms. "No, it's fine," she stated as she reached out and hugged me. "Congratulations."

I smelled the sweet fragrance of the flowers as she held them close.

"Thank you, Mom." I started to laugh. "We were so surprised. You should have seen James' face when the nurse told us."

My mom chuckled and pulled away from me. "I can imagine." She set the flowers on the windowsill. "I bet he's still stunned," she added, then inhaled deeply.

I watched her swallow hard and lick her lips.

"I brought something for you."

"Oh." I repositioned myself and swung my legs to the edge of the bed.

"No need to move. I'll bring it to you." Although the package was at the foot of my bed and I could have reached it, my mom picked it up and handed it to me. She stood back and watched as I opened it.

As I reached into the box, my mom took a hesitant step forward. I pulled out several cloth diapers. "Thanks, Mom."

"I'd made a few for you, but when I'd heard of the twins..." She wiped a tear from her eye. "I...I stayed up last night and made thirty of them. These are just a few. So, you don't have to worry about diapers."

What was different about her today? I'd expected her visit to be sterile like the sheets and white walls. "Wow, that's amazing. Thank you so much." I stroked a flannel lined, cloth diaper.

"Your dad has work he has to do and will swing by later. Do

you mind if I stay awhile, maybe even long enough to hold the girls?"

"Please, stay," I answered without pausing. "I'd like that."

Was there hope for us to mend the wall of tension we'd let build up between us?

CHAPTER 14

I folded the girls' outfits on the couch while I listened to the radio broadcast for the sunny July day. Feeling refreshed after a shower, I'd begun the laundry early in the morning before my mom stopped by for a visit and helped with the girls. Thankfully, both of them had fallen back to sleep after their early morning feeding and a window of time had opened for me.

These short bursts—when both girls slept—I thrived in completing tasks and staging for the next whirl of activity. I'd learned to compartmentalize my time to allow for the unexpected twists and turns of family life. Our girls were nine months old and could crawl all over the house. I held a sock to my chest and looked out the window. *Soon they'd be walking!* How could it be possible?

The rattle of the door interrupted my daydreaming, and I turned to see who was coming in.

"Hi, honey." My mom greeted me cheerfully as she shut the door. "Sorry, I'm a little late today." She walked to the couch and picked up an outfit, folding clothes while standing next to me. She'd been faithful in coming five days a week and helping with Brooke and Roberta.

Chapter 14

I smelled the vanilla perfume she wore religiously. Today, it brought me comfort to have the sweet scent tickle my nose. "It's okay, Mom."

"How are the girls today?" She asked as she placed the folded outfit on the chair next to her.

I picked up two sleepers, handed one to my mom, and held the other in my hand. "They were up early, ate, and fell right back to sleep."

My mom laughed. "They must be growing. I can hardly believe how much they're getting into things these last couple of weeks."

"Huh, I know. What will it be like when they are walking? I'll have to barricade the stairs, put rubber bands on the bathroom cupboards..." I let out a sigh.

"Oh, honey. It's only the beginning." My mom placed her arm on my shoulder.

I'd felt our relationship turn a corner these last nine months. The gap between us was narrowing.

"Mom?" I gulped and turned to face her.

"Yes?"

"Can I ask you a question about being a mom?" I stopped folding the clothes and searched her face.

She looked over at me. "Well, yes. Not sure I'll have the answer, but go for it."

"How can I be certain I'll have a good relationship with Roberta and Brooke eighteen years from now? Or thirty, for that matter?"

My mom brushed her auburn hair aside. "That's a good question. One I don't fully know how to answer. I do think it's long overdue that I tell you something. I've regretted the rough times I've had in my parenting. I've displaced my fears and failures on you, and it isn't fair. You've always reminded me so much of my brother who passed away. I haven't handled that well at all. But these last few months with you have been some of the happiest days of my life. So I guess there's always hope."

"I guess so."

"Can I tell you a little secret that has helped me as a mom?"

I saw the tears forming in my mom's eyes and nodded, still unsure where this was going.

"I've begun to express my feelings to God. About how I regretted the distance between us. I feel like He hears me. Just talking to Him gives me a bit of peace, knowing He's listening to my heart. I can't make sense of how my brother's death and your resemblance to him muddied the waters. It just did. I'm sorry." My mom dropped the clothes she had in her hand, put her arms around me, and cried softly.

"Thanks for sharing that with me, it means more than you know. And I've enjoyed our time together, too." I rubbed her shoulders and inhaled the sweet smell of her perfume. "Thanks, Mom."

She pulled away slowly and held my shoulders. "If you want to have a good relationship with Brooke and Roberta, I suggest you talk to God about it. Maybe you'll find some direction for your heart's desires."

I heard one of the girls fussing. I turned my head to the noise, then patted my mom's arm. "I'll try."

I walked with a purposeful stride to the hallway, encouraged by the knowledge that I could reach out to my mom and talk.

In the girls' room, I saw Roberta lying on her back in her crib, kicking her feet in her sleepers. She cooed at the mobile over her, and her smile widened when I leaned over the railing. Could life be any better than this?

"Hi, sunshine!" I whispered as I picked her up. As I spoke, I heard James' voice in the hall, and I tiptoed out of the room, holding Roberta and quietly shut the door behind me so I wouldn't awaken Brooke.

Chapter 14

"Yup, you guessed right." I heard James say as I walked down the hall.

My mom stood in the living room with a pile of clothes in her arms and her mouth wide open.

"What? What'd I miss?" I asked as I sat in the rocker in the corner with Roberta on my lap.

"Next month, at this time, we'll be heading back up the road, sweets." James flipped through some papers in his hand, oblivious to the blank stare my mom continued to give him.

"On to the next adventure. You know what they say: north to Alaska, north to the future." James walked over to me and took Roberta's little hand in his own. He spoke in his high-pitched voice to her. "You ready for igloos and icicles."

Roberta squealed.

"Oh, you like those, do you? Great! We'll let you grow to be a little bit bigger of a girl, and then we're off for more of Alaska."

I smiled at James and the gentle, tender ways he had with our girls. Alaska was not a surprise to me. We'd talked about going back. However, the look on my mom's face was difficult to see. I watched as the sadness lowered her shoulders and her movements slowed as she walked to the hall closet with the girls' clothes.

I looked up at James and hushed my voice. "I didn't know she'd respond like that."

"I could have softened the blow," he whispered. "I figured giving her a little notice would help, but maybe I made it worse."

James reached for Roberta and nestled her in his arms. His eyebrows gathered in, and he scrubbed a hand over his face, displaying the regret he felt for his blurted-out news.

Mom walked back into the living room and sat on the couch with her hands folded on her lap.

"I'm sorry. I should have been more sensitive," James stated and he stood up, handing Roberta to my mom.

She picked up a burp rag next to her and held Roberta close to her shoulder, patting her back. "I forgive you. I'll try and enjoy every moment I can." The tears in her eyes flowed down her cheeks, but she held a smile on her face.

If my daughter had just told me she was moving, I'd feel torn too. The joy of having my girls and then seeing them off would be almost too much to bear. Was it the right choice? Leaving family behind again? Leaving the bonds we'd strengthened with time? Leaving the bounty of help I'd had at my side all these months? Perhaps I should talk to God about it.

But where would I start?

I stood up from the rocker and walked to the kitchen to make coffee. Some coffee, some conversation, and maybe a card game, and we'd all laugh a little. There would be time to sort it out.

Or would the next few weeks be too much, knowing we were going again?

CHAPTER 15

WE'D DRIVEN STALWARTLY TO FAIRBANKS, determined to reach the city with our sanity intact after almost a week on the road with our ten-month-old girls.

The rain intensified on this chilly August afternoon as we neared Tok, a small rural town only a few hours away from the hustle and bustle of Fairbanks.

"I like this little place," James stated as he drove the Volkswagen bus we'd purchased for our trip into the customs parking lot.

Although we were ninety miles from the border, the official customs stop was in Tok. It appeared to be a hub for the area, with a gas station and a grocery store.

"What do you like about it?" I asked, turning in my seat to check on the girls, who I'd laid to sleep on the mattress in the back a couple of hours ago.

James turned the vehicle off and leaned on the steering wheel. "I guess I prefer the small towns along the way to the city. I wonder why each person is here. What brought them? What's their story?"

I'd wondered as well, when we'd passed through locations on the highways with scatterings of people hundreds of miles from the nearest city. What would it be like to live in such a remote area without amenities like hospitals and shopping malls?

In the parking lot, a little family scurried to the corner to cross the highway, dodging the rain. I assumed it was a mom with her three children. They looked both ways, then proceeded.

Fussing from the back caught my attention, and I shifted in my seat to look. Which of the girls was awake? Brooke was directly behind me, and she squirmed. She was one to place her favorite blanket on her head when she slept. I tugged it down off her shoulders, revealing her flushed face and sweaty, matted hair.

More moaning, and then she thrashed and kicked her feet.

"Brooke, settle down." I reached to touch her so she wouldn't roll off the edge of the mattress.

"Do you want to take the girls inside or stay in the van?" James asked as he pulled his coat from between our bucket seats.

I maneuvered from the front of the van as I answered him. "I'll stay in here with the girls and give them something to eat."

"Okay," James said as he shut his door.

In the back, I rearranged our bags and groceries so I could place Brooke on my lap while her fussing intensified. As I picked her up, the heat from her little body radiated through her thin clothes. She shouldn't be so warm.

"Shh, Brooke."

Roberta fussed next to me, and I looked from one girl to the other. How long would James be?

"It's okay, Roberta. I'm here." I touched her belly, and she yawned, stretching her arms up.

We'd figured simple clothing would be best for the girls on the car ride and that we'd get outfits when we arrived in Fairbanks. Brooke's outfit was drenched in the back, and I unzipped her sleeper.

Chapter 15

Had James turned the heat up?

The rain outside pelted on the roof and the noise of it hitting the metal was deafening.

"Okay, Brooke, Mommy has you." I held her in her diaper and stood her up so the air would cool her warm skin. She continued to cry, but her intensity lessened just as Roberta's increased. I felt torn between them, stuffed amidst our things like a sardine in a tin can. My mother or James had almost always been near when they cried simultaneously. Maybe I should cry? The idea zinged through my mind like a bolt of lightning. How silly would it look to James when he got back? All three of us crying with only a few hours left of our trip.

"Girls, we need to get it together," I stated to my infants, who'd no clue what I meant.

As I finished speaking, a knock on the side door jolted me, and I froze. I could barely see the figure outside, wet with rain. Should I open the door? Figuring this small town offered little risk in front of the US Border Patrol, I opened the door as best I could, bracing Brooke on my lap.

A man in green slickers and a Stetson hat stood outside the van. "Hi, ma'am. I'm a state trooper. My office is inside. Did you want to come in while your husband finishes the paperwork? He asked if I'd check on you." He squinted, searching the van with his eyes. "Looks like you have your hands full here."

"Yeah, it'd be easier to stay here than try and get inside at this point. Thanks though." I cleared my throat as he shut the door.

What had washed over me, to consider moving away from the support of my mom? Her devotion to us was the least expected and ended up being the most appreciated. My decision-making must have been skewed by the ease she provided through her care of the girls. Why hadn't I noted the mountain-sized help she'd brought to our family? I'd also overlooked my dad's character. Our time together cast a spotlight on his enduring support of both James and me. There wasn't enough of me at the moment, never mind when the girls started walking.

Looking from Brooke to Roberta, I shook my head as they both cried, demanding all of me. I redressed Brooke now that her skin had cooled. Then I laid her on my lap and reached for Roberta, who had one leg drawn out of her sleeper and caught in the torso of her outfit. One daughter would have to wait for the other.

I'd have to learn how to set myself aside because there wasn't room for me. Still, I'd need help. James would start school in a matter of weeks. Surely in as large a city as Fairbanks, I'd find something.

THE STRAIGHT ROAD IN FRONT OF US LED THE WAY TO the Golden Heart City of Fairbanks. We'd traveled the last fifty miles of the Richardson Highway in silence. Thankfully, the rain had subsided after we left Delta, nearly a hundred miles ago. However, a storm was brewing within our VW van.

"What were we thinking? Why did we think we were up for more adventure?" I said with tears in my eyes, my mind second-guessing every mile since we'd left Tok.

"It's the long trip. I feel it too, Sharon. We've got to have enough resolve to see it through. In no time, we'll be laughing with friends over Thanksgiving dinner."

I'd stayed in the back for the rest of the trip so I could juggle the girls. The distance from where I sat to where James gripped the wheel might as well have been the thousands of miles we'd traveled from home because he wasn't hearing my heart.

The van couldn't travel fast enough to our new place, blocks from Nordale School, where James had taught previously. There was unpacking to do, baths for all of us and grocery shopping. I felt my chest tighten at the enormity of what the rest of the day held. I tried to look out the window to see what I recognized.

"Did you hear me about Thanksgiving?" James said as he looked over his shoulder briefly.

"James, I can hardly see past today," I stated as I gazed down at the girls who'd fallen asleep after some food, diaper changes, and a snuggle.

"I'm sorry, sweets. I try to help, and I fail miserably. I want you to be happy. When we get settled, we'll find someone to watch the girls and we'll go out for a nice dinner. You deserve a break after this long trip."

He was trying, and I guess, together, we were attempting to make life's chances fall into place smoothly.

I looked over at the girls who now slept on the mattress, and I repositioned the blanket over them. "Okay, James. I'm sorry, too, for being impatient."

Why hadn't I tried to see what this moment might look like when I'd casually said yes to our return? It wasn't Alaska; it was me. Where would I fit into the continuation of our Alaskan adventure?

CHAPTER 16

I FOUND PLACES TO WALK WITH THE GIRLS DURING the day while the sun still held late-August warmth. Brooke and Roberta seemed to enjoy being outside in the baby buggy I'd discovered at a yard sale. Thankfully, another family with twins wasn't in need of the oversized contraption any longer. James and I were frugal with our funds, and when I came across something affordable that would make my life easier, I considered it a precious jewel.

The girls kicked and cooed as I shifted the buggy shade to block the sunshine from their faces. "You like walks, don't you?" I said as I leaned down closer to them.

Their faces lit up with wide smiles, and Brooke blew a bubble with her saliva.

"We should go see your daddy and walk home with him."

"Da, da, da." I heard one of them say, and I shook my head, recalling how ecstatic James had been when he'd first heard them say, "da."

He'd jumped up in place and placed his palm over his heart. His girls, they had him in the palms of their hands.

We'd walked to the bird sanctuary called Creamer's Field in hopes of seeing some migratory geese passing through on their

Chapter 16

journey south. The noise of birds overhead caught my attention, and I held my hand to my forehead, blocking the bright light to see if I could recognize what kind they were.

During our two-mile walk, I'd taken in the sights and scents of the fall season of the north. "Look girls!" I pointed up as I squatted next to the buggy. "It's a flock of geese! They're flying south, down to Grandma's."

Brooke and Roberta were oblivious to my announcement, but smiled at my cheery voice and clenched their small hands. Roberta tried to roll over. I watched them tussle in the small space and swallowed the lump in my throat as a wave of sadness flooded me. Why had I mentioned Grandma?

I stood up and turned the cart to begin our walk back to our basement apartment near Nordale School.

The geese held to a pattern. Their sense of time and temperature guided them to fly away and home. I didn't have a pattern. Where was my reference point? I looked around at the other people walking nearby. Did they have a set way of living out life?

I gulped again and pasted a smile on my face as I peeked down at the girls, who kept each other entertained. I'd need some sense of direction to pass on to them. My mom had admitted she'd lost her way in raising me. She'd displaced her emotions. I didn't want to emulate that pattern from generation to generation.

A young couple walked toward me, arm in arm. The woman threw her head back in laughter, oblivious to the fact that she was about to run into the baby buggy. Her beau shifted her closer to himself a second before we had a collision and nodded to me as they passed.

Had I been lost in my own world like she had?

After the forty-five-minute walk, the school came into view, and I pulled back my long sleeve shirt to see the time on my watch. "All right, girls, let's go see Daddy set up his classroom." I'd fallen into a habit of visiting James when his workday ended, and we'd walked home together. Maybe there was something else I could add to my week to bring a sense of stability and belonging?

I pushed the buggy down the hall and scanned the rooms as I walked. Most of the classrooms looked ready for the return of students after Labor Day weekend. It wouldn't be long before James would be engrossed with paperwork and lesson plans. Taking a deep breath, I rounded the corner into his room at the end of the hall.

"Here come my girls!" James called out from his desk. He rose from his chair and scurried to the buggy. He gave me a kiss on the cheek before he leaned over and picked up Brooke. "Guess I should have been quieter so I didn't wake them up. Looks like Roberta is still asleep. How was your walk today?"

I brushed back some loose hair from my face. "Great. We saw lots of geese. Winter must be quickly approaching. They seemed to follow a beacon south."

Back at his desk, James propped Brooke up on his knees and spoke to her. "You're getting so strong." He lifted her up and down, touching her feet to his legs. "Before I forget, another teacher invited us to their place for dinner Friday."

"Oh?" I replied as I rocked the buggy in hopes of keeping Roberta asleep.

"Brad and his wife have folks over every Friday for tacos. He said the visits are a highlight of their week. Want to go? They live in North Pole, which means we can have a pleasant drive out of the city every week if we become regulars." James sat Brooke down on his lap, facing him.

"Wow, that sounds great. I was just thinking on my walk of how I'd like to add something to my week." I pushed the buggy over to James' desk and placed my hand on his shoulder.

We both laughed as Brooke cooed in surprise at her own hiccups.

There would soon be a weekly rhythm with a prize at the

end—visiting new friends. I smiled at James and kissed his cheek.

"Oh, you'll have to visit my class more often if I get a little sugar like that." He stood up, placed Brooke back in the buggy, and gave me a hug, pulling me in close.

I inhaled the fragrance of his aftershave and savored his embrace. We traveled some bumpy roads at times, like any couple. I hoped we moved in step as a loving couple, giving our girls the security they deserved.

I PLACED THE BOWL ON THE COUNTER NEAR THE SINK. I wanted to make a homemade salsa to take for taco night at our new friends' house. This would be our second week spending the evening with Brad and his wife Jean, along with their other friends who came to taco time each week. Perhaps one of these weeks we could invite everyone to our place.

I looked around our small basement apartment. What was I thinking? Of course we couldn't. We hardly had enough room for ourselves and the twins in our one-bedroom rental. However, maybe we could all meet somewhere, like a park for a cookout. Or we could go sledding in the winter when the girls were bigger.

I heard James' friendly whistle in the hall and then the door opened. I moved from the galley kitchen to see him coming in the doorway with one girl in each arm. He'd gone on a short walk with them while we still had some above-freezing temperatures in mid-September.

"Sharon," he stated as he walked in. His flat voice alerted me, and I wiped my hands on the apron tied at my waist.

"What is it?" I walked closer and took Roberta from him.

"She's extra fussy today."

Had he only wanted me to take her from his arms or was

there more? I studied his face for a clue. "Oh?"

After slipping his shoes off, James walked with Brooke to the living room and sat on the couch. "She cried almost the whole time."

I kissed Roberta on the cheek, and she wriggled in my arms. "What is it, baby girl?"

"Maybe she's extra hungry or something?"

With Roberta on my hip, I moved back to the kitchen and pulled the peppers and onions out of the fridge. Roberta fussed, and I opened the fridge again to pull out the half-drunk bottle I'd placed in there earlier.

"I'll warm up some milk for her then, even though it's early."

I turned the faucet on and let it run while I pulled out a glass from the cupboard. I placed the glass in the sink, letting the warm water fill the cup, and then I submerged the bottle.

"Where'd you walk to?" I asked, as I moved into the living room to sit by James and Brooke.

James scooted over near the arm of the couch to make room for us. "Oh, you know. The usual. I march them down the block and then I march them back again. We do a few wheelies with the mighty buggy, and I time how long they can go on autopilot with a quick little push and so forth."

I gasped and turned to face him. "What?"

He laughed and tossed Brooke into the air. "Me and the girls, we have our fun. Just don't you worry."

Truthfully, I did worry. I worried about so many things lately. I pulled Roberta's sweater off and set it on the arm of the couch. "Okay, James," I replied as I held my gaze on Roberta. "I'll try not to."

He leaned closer to me and turned my chin so I faced him. "I was only joking. I walk around the block twice."

I gave him a quick smile and then pulled Roberta close to soothe her fussing. "James?"

"Yes, sweets?" He stood up and placed Brooke on a blanket

Chapter 16

on the floor, where she kicked and cooed. Then he sat next to me and put his arm around me.

"Do you worry about anything?" I asked, wondering, and hoping there were things weighing him down so I didn't feel like a deserted boat bobbing in the middle of ocean.

James rubbed my shoulder as he spoke. "Of course I do. I worry all season long if Michigan will beat Ohio in football."

I rolled my eyes and pulled ahead to stand, but he held me back with his arm.

"Sorry," he said. "Sure, I do. As the man of the house, I think about providing for you and the girls. Good grief, it wasn't even a year ago that we'd assumed we were about to have a busy little boy, and here we are a family of four!"

As though on cue, Roberta's cries increased in volume.

I handed her to James. "I'll go get her bottle." I moved to the kitchen and cleared my throat. Pulling the bottle from the now-lukewarm water, I gave it a gentle shake and then tested the milk on my wrist.

"Uh, sweets?" I heard James' awkward voice.

I reached for a glass of water to satiate my dry throat. "What?"

"Can you come here? Quick!"

With a bottle in one hand and my glass in the other, I stepped swiftly into the living room. James held Roberta out at arm's length and was covered in a pool of puke that ran down the front of his shirt to his lap. A look of disgust swept across his face with a scrunched nose.

"Hurry, Sharon...I'm...going...to..." His voice trailed off as he gagged.

I turned and set the bottle on the counter along with the glass and scurried to grab Roberta from his arms. "Come here, you poor baby!" Using my apron, I wiped her face and went to the bathroom to grab a rag.

"Sharon!" James called out to me.

"Just a second," I answered as I pulled off Roberta's outfit and tossed it in the tub to rinse out later. I looked her over from head to toe, wondering what could be wrong and fretting that it might be something serious.

Roberta pushed back at me and cried harder. Over her wailing, I could hear James' comments about the stench. Then Brooke let out a cry.

Going back to the living room, I set Roberta down on a blanket. She'd have to wait.

I burst out in laughter at the sight of James, covered in Roberta's vomit—one hand over his eyes and the other pinching his nose.

He widened his fingers, looking at me through the small slit it made. "Funny, real funny," he said. "If you want to worry about anything, you could worry about getting me off this island in the middle of a pool of puke."

With both girls now crying louder with each second, I reached for a flannel blanket on a nearby chair and wiped the mess from James' lap as best I could. "You've been christened, James."

"And you better hurry, ugh"—he wretched—"before I christen you." He stood up, holding the blanket tight across his waist, and scurried to the bathroom.

I placed my hands on my hips and surveyed the mess all around me. So much for fresh salsa and tacos with friends on a Friday night.

Was there a recipe to cure the worry that crept in at moments like these? Times as a parent when you didn't know if your baby was okay and you sensed everything could unravel?

I bit at my lip, untied my messy apron, and wadded it into a ball. Mom had said to try talking to God. The suggestion crept upon me like a cat on a mouse. A notion to consider amid the mess and crying babies.

God? Where do I find help?

CHAPTER 17

IN THE FIRST WEEK OF OCTOBER, WE CELEBRATED THE girl's first birthday by having cake and playing in the freshly fallen snow. On Thanksgiving, we were entertained by their first steps around our small apartment. By Christmas, Brooke's and Roberta's personalities had begun to rise to the surface like bubbles in a glass of champagne.

That night was New Year's Eve, and we planned to usher it in with my brother John, who'd made the trip north during the darkest and coldest part of the year. Time with family was welcome, no matter the occasion or the season.

John was clowning around with the twins at the breakfast table when the black rotary phone rang. James stood up to answer the call in the living room.

"Good morning," James stated.

I stood up from the table, tightened my robe around my waist, picked up my coffee mug, and poured myself some of the fresh brew from the pot on the counter. The dark mornings of winter invited me to linger on the couch with coffee and ease into the day, especially over the holidays.

"What's the plan for today?" John questioned as I set my mug down and lifted Brooke from her spot at the table.

"Not much until this evening." I moved to the sink and grabbed a rag to wipe the girls' hands.

"Remember when we'd stay up late putting puzzles together on New Year's?" John asked as he stood up and bent over to pick up Roberta and carry her closer to me.

I washed Roberta's face, and she wiggled in John's arms. "I'd forgotten about that. We'd race to get them done before Christmas break was over."

"Maybe we could find one to do while I'm here."

The thought of staying up late and visiting with John was inviting. "Sure, we can walk down to the grocery store later. They have some."

John set Roberta down, and the girls waddled into the living room, gabbing to one another in their own little language.

"It's so funny watching them," John stated as he began to clear the table. "They are so much alike, yet so different."

"Uh-huh, I know. Brooke seems to take command, and yet Roberta finds a way to poke back. They laugh at one another all the time, like they have these inside jokes."

John held his belly as though he were laughing. "I noticed that Roberta takes her time with a task, like she's trying to figure it out." He narrowed his eyes, squinting. "Brooke tunes into facial expressions and mimics them when playing with her dolls." He held up his hands and motioned like he was a mime touching an invisible wall.

I chuckled at his imitations. "They are really different. But they often act as one, like when they mirror each other and do the same motion in unison."

"Alrighty," James said as he hung up the phone. "Does anyone want to go and watch the fireworks tonight?"

"Yes," John and I said together and laughed.

"You're like the girls, answering the same thing at the same time," he said, smiling. "Brad invited us to come to North Pole and join them for the New Year's festivities they have there."

Chapter 17

"Sure," I answered, happy to have an outing away from the usual.

We cleaned up from breakfast and passed the time on our lazy morning, visiting. I couldn't help but savor the time with my brother and smile at his playful banter with James. I sensed I'd tuck these memories away to enjoy long after John went back home, early next week.

I pulled back the curtains in the living room to see the pink hues in the sky painting the wisps of clouds. Winter had a way of gripping me on so many levels. It brought back memories of our wedding, our first winter in Fairbanks, and the transitions of our life together over the past three years.

Once again, looking out at the snow drifts and watching the flakes fall under the glow of the streetlights, I felt like we lived in a snow globe and someone had picked us up and given us a shake.

"Wanna go for that walk to the store, Ronnie?" John asked from the kitchen.

"Sure. James, are you okay here with the girls?" I reached down and picked up one of the socks the girls had pulled off their feet.

"Most definitely. The girls and I have some dancing to do with Mr. Music here in a half hour." James shuffled from the eating area to the living room, then started his own jig and hummed.

Brooke started clapping and Roberta giggled.

I moved toward the hallway. "Ha, looks like they are in good hands."

When John and I were about halfway to the store, he slipped on the ice and grabbed at my arm. We slid around, laughing and trying to stand upright.

"I need cleats to walk," John stated. "How do you do it? You've acclimated to the conditions here. I must admit, I'm a little jealous of how much you've eased into your Alaskan life."

I brushed the snow from my mittens. "Hardly."

"You don't see it, but you're awfully casual about being outside in the cold and taking the girls out in their big puffy winter gear." He waddled along as though he were overstuffed, just like the girls did when they were all bundled up.

"James and I really like it. We've talked about going to other parts of the state too," I added as we shuffled across the crosswalk, careful to avoid the ice patches that led to the other side of the street. "Have any New Year's resolutions?" I questioned John, who sketched drawings of his new resolutions every year, then used them as posters for his wall like a well-thought-out battle plan.

"Yeah, work a little harder at finding a wife," he said matter-of-factly.

I laughed out loud, then sobered. "Sorry, it's not funny." I touched his elbow with my mitten. "These things just happen; we don't always *work* for them."

"All right. I have more. Maybe it's part of getting older and inching closer to thirty. I wonder what I'll leave behind. Like you? Do you have goals and aspirations as a parent? Any kind of legacy you hope to give your girls?" He held my elbow as we inched around a pile of snow blocking the alleyway next to a store.

I looked down at my feet as I tiptoed around an icy patch on the sidewalk. "Not sure. I started with the thought of simply being a good parent, and now that they're toddlers, it's keeping them alive every day without a major accident."

"Deeper. You need to dig deeper. What will they remember you for?" John challenged.

His query was inspirational, yet tough to ponder. What would they see in me? Were there admirable qualities I could share with them? I saw James as the outgoing adventure-seeker and myself as the faithful sidekick. But as an individual, who was I?

Chapter 17

We reached the store, and John opened the door for me. "Think about it."

"I will," I answered. Then I wandered back in time to the resolve I had to learn more about raising my girls and my determination to keep them safe.

After walking around the grocery store for a minute, we found the toy aisle and searched through the puzzles.

What piece of the puzzle would I bring to the family? We were each important, but what role did I play? John's probing was valuable. I knew I wanted to be a good mom but the word *good* was subjective. I was with my girls and cared for them. What more could I offer?

As we waited to check out, I fidgeted with my zipper and John looked at the outdoorsy Alaska magazines. Following him through the line, I considered what kind of a New Year's resolution I could work on. Was there someone I should aim to be more like? Someone whose example I should follow? My mind was blank. I was stumped on how to dig deeper, as John had suggested.

We left the store and headed out into the snow globe. I rubbed my forearms to get the blood moving before I put my mittens back on and lifted my hood up on my head.

A season of change was on the northern horizon. I could feel it. Maybe this new year would bring its own way for me to figure out who I was and mold me into who I needed to be.

CHAPTER 18

We bundled up the girls in their winter gear and loaded into our VW van to go and watch the dog sled races on a bright, but cold, afternoon in March.

In early January, when John was still visiting, we explored the unique activities hosted in Fairbanks and the surrounding area. James and I aspired to show the girls as much of the arctic culture as we could. When I told my parents about our adventures, I could hear my mom shudder over the phone. "You're braver than I am. I'd be watching from my car."

I didn't see myself as courageous—I simply wanted to face the opportunities we had and share them as a family.

"Do you suppose they'll have the blanket toss after the dog derbies like they did last time?" I asked James as we pulled into the parking lot at Creamer's Field. Numerous vehicles were parked perpendicular to the wooden fence that lined the snowy track.

"I hope so. Folks tossing someone in the air with a seal hide is a sight to see. It's like a people-powered trampoline."

"Do you know anything about where the tradition comes from?"

James was endlessly curious about Alaskan culture and

Chapter 18

researched everything we came across. I could always count on him to have an explanation. He had a teacher's heart.

"I sure do. I was just telling the kids in school this week that the blanket toss originated among Alaskan and Canadian natives. They used it as a way to sight whales as they hunted."

James turned off the van, and I turned in my seat to see both girls had fallen asleep on the short drive.

"A hunting technique?" I whispered "That is genius." I moved closer to James. "I guess I'll watch from here until the girls wake up. This morning's dancing with you must have wore them out."

"I'll sit here with you. Want to play a little game of chance while we watch?" James asked.

I chuckled. "Not really. Do you still believe chance is what draws us to the paths we take?"

"I was only joking about the game, my sweets." He pulled his gloves off and set them on his lap. "I'm not sure what spirals us in one direction or the next. There's so much out there to explore. How else do you decide?"

I unzipped my oversized coat, pulled my arms out of the sleeves, and placed the fluffy bundle on my lap. "I trust there's more out there than what we can see. We both grew up in church. Do you think God could have a hand, even in the big items?"

James nodded. "Yes, I believe God and chance are both true. If we leave life's decisions to chance, then, in theory, wouldn't God see to it that we have what it takes to accept the natural consequences, good or bad?" He shrugged. "But it's not just about throwing things into the wind. Planning plays a part too. It can help us overcome small disruptions and disappointments." He reached for my hand. "That's where you shine. You're excellent at organizing and tending to small details."

I smiled at his compliment. "I try to anticipate how I should react, but in the moment, I don't follow through. For example, when we decided to come here, inside, I was like, *Yes let's do this.*"

I gave him a thumbs up. "Then doubt surfaces when it doesn't all perfectly line up."

"In my opinion, you've been a great sport about rolling the dice and taking it all in. I look forward to many years of adventures ahead." He leaned closer, whispering, "You're doing a great job." He kissed me softly. "There's not much that could derail things. Just look at us. We've got these girls tag-teamed, and they can fall sleep at the sound of the van's ignition." He snapped his fingers.

Appreciating James' enthusiasm and optimism, I warmed to his idea of *hopeful* planning. I gently bit at my lip and smiled, willing myself to believe everything would be all right so I could set aside the worry that grew within me at the slightest change in the girls or our situation. It wasn't anxiety but the unsettled feeling of uncertainty.

"Do you want to go and watch closer while I stay with girls?" James offered.

"Sure."

I attempted to quietly open the coat folded on my lap. The rough fabric crinkled in my hands, and I stopped to look back at the girls. Roberta had her eyes open and was rubbing her ear.

"Actually, let's all go. "We have one awake, and I'm sure it won't hurt for us to pick up Brooke and bring her. Maybe she'll keep napping on your shoulder," I said.

The January air was frigid against my face, but the beauty of the winter sky was breathtaking. The sunrises and sunsets we had at this time of year painted the skies for the majority of the day.

Once we had both girls situated, we walked along the fence toward the finish line where mushers worked with their dog teams to be ready for the races.

Roberta started barking like a dog when we got closer to the lineup. "Puppy," she said, pointing in front of her.

I squatted next to her and talked to her about the dogs. "See, the puppy has boots on, just like you."

"Boo?" she said and looked down at her own feet.

We watched the dog handlers harness the dogs and help align the sleds. Some dogs barked and others howled as the excitement grew—the race about to start. I'd learned about dog sledding since our first visit to the track, and I knew the dogs loved to pull and were genuinely excited about the races. It was such a treat to watch them run. I'd developed an appreciation for how Balto, the famous sled dog, had helped carry the medicine to the city of Nome to help sick children a little over forty years ago.

"Puppy pull," Brooke said and raised her eyebrows.

"Yes, they love to pull. See how happy they are?" I asked. I pointed to a dog team where the lead dog was already straining at his harness, excited to begin.

"But puppy needs to work with his team and be patient," I added. *Huh, just like me.* I needed patience during the uncertain times. It wasn't enough to show my girls the events around town. I had to be an example to them. I had to show them a steady display of care and concern. Would I have enough of both to pass on?

When we got back to our apartment, I pulled the mail out of the box and brought it in with me while James stayed in the front yard with the girls in the snow.

In the stack of mail was an envelope from Mary. I tore at the back tab and opened it. Inside was a beautiful card with a picture of Stan Hywet Hall & Gardens. My eyes stung with tears. She knew how much I loved visiting the historic Akron house and museum, along with the gardens and greenhouse. It was thoughtful of her to remember. I opened the card and read it out loud to myself.

Dear Sharon,

I miss you and James so much, but especially the girls. In a strange turn of events, my summer has opened up, and I can come and spend an extended amount of time with you if you'd like. I know James has taken on some seasonal work between school years, so I figured the timing might be perfect. Please give me an honest answer because I want my visit to be a help and not a hindrance. I'll bring anything from here you might still be missing. I look forward to hearing from you.

Love, Mary

I DABBED THE TEARS FROM MY EYES. I'D BEEN GIVEN such a kind and generous family. Of course I'd answer yes, unless James saw reason not to.

When I'd first seen Mary's name on the card, the hollow feeling of homesickness had pulled my shoulders down. Now with the anticipation of her extended visit, I felt inspired to find ways to explore Fairbanks together. It would be a summer to remember.

CHAPTER 19

BROOKE AND ROBERTA SHARED A BLUEBERRY MUFFIN at the small table while Mary and I lingered over our raspberry scone. The Fairbanks airport bustled with activity as we awaited the last call for Mary's flight.

"You're doing so well with the girls. It's hard to believe they'll turn two in a couple of months," Mary stated as she brushed some crumbs from the front of her shirt into the palm of her hand. "I never doubt you'd be an amazing mom. It's just been so wonderful to be a part of your summer, stacking up memories together."

The busy days didn't leave much room for reflection, especially with two active toddlers. "Thanks, I'm trying." Honestly, without her help, I don't know how I would have handled summer while James was busy with his extra job during the break from school.

Mary leaned toward the girls in their stroller and handed them each a brochure that she'd picked up from the display stand earlier. "Look at these pretty pictures." She pointed to the inside. "So, what do you think is next for you guys? Any big plans for the future? Going to roll some dice soon and spice things up a bit?" She giggled.

"Oh, mercy, no more dice-rolling. We don't have any change of plans. Well, not that I know of. I'd like to think we'll be here for a bit." I picked up the brochure that Roberta had dropped on the floor and now squealed at as she tried to reach it.

"Well, you never know. Just when we least expect it, life seems to toss us around. I'm speaking for myself now. I'd like to see if I can get a different apartment this fall and maybe join a bowling league." As she finished speaking, the announcement for her flight came over the speaker. She looked at her watch. "Guess it's time, sis."

I reached for Mary's hand. "That sounds fun, something good to look forward to. I need some of that in my life too." The tears I was holding back slid from the corner of my eye. "And, hey, thanks again for coming."

Mary avoided eye contact, squatted next to the girls, and hugged each of them, then stood to embrace me in a tight hug. "Goodbye."

"Bye," I whispered and dabbed my eyes with the sleeve of my shirt.

The flood of emotions washing over me as I waved goodbye to Mary was what I'd hoped to avoid. Her summer help had been a gift that I wasn't sure I could ever repay. We'd spent countless hours with the girls on walks and at parks. Brooke and Roberta, now twenty-two months old, had gabbed in gibberish almost non-stop to one another during our prolonged goodbye. My heart felt so torn at the contrast between my sorrow and their gaiety. They waved and grinned at Mary from their stroller as she stepped onto the airport breezeway.

"Okay, girls, let's get back to the car and see if we can go home and dry out."

The incessant rain from the last couple of days of August was unlike anything I'd experienced growing up in the Midwest when heavy storms meant tornadoes were lingering close by. It had rained for almost a week now, and I'd overheard locals at

Chapter 19

the grocery store mention they'd never seen anything quite like it.

Back at the apartment, I hung up our wet coats while the girls walked to their toy bin in the corner. They were a delight to watch in their stage of exploration. James called them "twenty-hands," as they held onto one object and grabbed at others nearby. I turned on the radio in the corner to hear the local news, which would air in a few brief minutes. I sat on the couch, watching the girls, and smiled at their cheerful ways. Pride swelled within me as I thought of Mary's reminder: *they're almost two!*

The announcer caught my attention with the words "Life is unfair and unmanageable. People are unreliable. And your future is unpredictable."

What a downer.

I picked up some paper that I'd set down next to the couch earlier. I'd recently taken up origami, and I hung the little folded creations in our small windows.

I froze at the next sentence spoken by the radio broadcaster. "Are you dissatisfied? You need to admit the source of your frustration. Otherwise, you are a fugitive from your own destiny."

Mesmerized with the sermon, I stood and inched closer—as though the radio were alive. "Admit to God that you have a need for Him in this nonsense world."

When I reached the stereo, I turned it down and moved toward the couch and spoke out loud to Brooke and Roberta.

"Grandma told me I should talk to God. What do you girls think?" I squatted next to them as they flipped through some board books. "What would I tell Him? I know! I could count for Him. One, two and three." I held up three fingers. "One, I know my future is unpredictable. Ha, I'm married to your daddy!"

"Daddy," Brooke said, sitting straighter and then putting her little book on the carpet.

"Yes, your daddy. He's very unpredictable, but I'd rather say he's adventurous. Okay, two, I am dissatisfied. That leads me to number three. I'd ask, How does God help make sense of the nonsense?"

Roberta clapped and then stood up as though I had given a great speech, and I laughed. Then I caught the word "news" from the stereo and jumped to turn up the volume. We'd been listening closely for reports of possible flooding, and James had made me promise I'd stay on top of it.

"...higher ground. Half an hour ago, the flood waters crested the Chena River banks."

I clasped my mouth. Our worst fear was that the waters would rise to levels that were unmanageably high.

"Oh, God! What do we do?" I searched the room as though the answer were near.

When the news report was over, I went to the kitchen to make some coffee. I needed to keep myself busy so I wouldn't wallow in worry or show the girls the fear that welled up within me.

James burst through the door to the apartment and froze in place in the living room. "Did you hear?" He scooped up Brooke and walked her over to me, placing her in my arms.

"Honey, what are you doing here?" I questioned as I walked over to give him a kiss hello.

The girls shouted "Daddy!" and waved at him, and he went to give them each a hug and a kiss.

"They said the river is flooding. I hurried home to be with you." He walked to our small window and pulled back the curtain. "I'll go ask Gary what to do. We haven't lived here long enough to know if we're in imminent danger or not."

James turned on his heels and headed back out the door as quick as he'd arrived.

"Brooke and Roberta," I stated with my hands across my abdomen. "Let's pray."

I stood in the living room and talked to God. "Will you please

Chapter 19

keep us safe?" I opened my eyes, which I had shut, and looked down at my two girls, then I closed them again. "We need help to manage it all. Amen."

Did He hear me?

Not sure what else to say or do, I walked back to the kitchen, put the coffee percolator under the tap and filled it. As I stood there, lost in my own contemplation of which direction to turn, the water overfilled the container and spilled into the sink.

JAMES AND OUR LANDLORD, GARY, RETURNED TO OUR apartment with strict instructions to head to the upper level of the building. There wasn't time to grab much other than Brooke and Roberta.

"What are you going to do?" I asked James as he moved sheets of plywood from the hallway into the apartment.

"We're going to board up the windows. I'll be up when we're done." He pulled more supplies into our apartment and gave me a gentle push into the hall.

"Head to safety, sweets," he said as he kissed my cheek.

"C'mon girls." I ushered them into the hall, pulling the little wagon we used for long walks.

I'd piled their diapers in around them and they smiled, patting the piles. Did they imagine we were going on an adventure outside?

Once we were upstairs, the landlord's wife, Liza, welcomed us in.

I pulled the wagon into the middle of the room. Liza's little girl sat on the floor, looking at magazines. From this vantage point, the rain sounded like a torrent out to ravage the building.

"Thanks. Wow, the rain is so loud up here," I stated as I took each of the girls out of the wagon.

"I think what you're hearing is the rushing water as well." Liza noted as she moved toward the window.

Rushing water? Was it gaining enough of a forceable momentum to do harm in such a short amount of time? My heart raced, and I looked out the window at the back alley. The water poured through the street, not in a trickle, but in a gushing torrent, as though from a broken dam.

"I had no clue," I said, as I watched the muddy water rise. Stunned by its momentum, I breathed a prayer out loud. "Thank God we had somewhere to go and that James arrived when he did."

"God?" Liza questioned. "Where's He in all of this?" She waved her hand in front of her.

Perhaps she was right.

"And the guys better hurry," she mumbled as she walked back to her little girl, who was now ripping out magazine pages.

Roberta and Brooke wobbled around the room, exploring, and I followed their steps, watching their feet as they moved. How'd our adventure turn sour so quickly? Where was the help we needed? Who could stop the force of the water? Certainly, an army was ready, somewhere, to battle the waves? Didn't cities have plans in place for such things? Back home, tornadoes came with a vengeance, but we had root cellars and shelters.

"Is there a flood brigade here?" I asked Liza. "Or something like it?"

"I haven't lived here long, but I know Fairbanks isn't known for flooding. Usually, it's still hot this time of year, not pouring rain."

My girls were oblivious, oohing at their new surroundings and touching the couches, chairs, and end tables set up in the large room. Brooke sat down, ran her hand along the shag rug on the floor, and then lay down on it. She didn't know a storm raged outside. The presence of her mom was all she needed to feel safe.

Chapter 19

The door to the apartment opened, and James and the landlord walked in.

"I don't know how long those efforts will hold, but at least we did what we could," James said as he walked over to the side of the room where I was with the girls.

Suddenly, a noise arose that reminded me of the powerful winds preceding a tornado. But where was it coming from? I rushed at Brooke and picked her up off the floor. The roaring sound increased, and I huddled next to James, who held Roberta in his arms. Air rushed up from under us, billowing out of the air vents in the floor, and the curtains blew away from the walls.

"Oh, God!" I cried out and pushed myself against James. He held me with his free arm, and his grip strengthened.

"The plywood must not have held up to the water," James said matter-of-factly.

I inhaled deeply and searched James' face. "What?"

James' face stiffened. "I'm guessing that was a force of air from the water breaking through the cement blocks."

"Through what?" I asked as I pulled Brooke's hand away from her grasp on my hair.

"The walls," Gary stated. "I'll get on the handheld radio." He moved closer to James. "We're going to have to get everyone out as fast as possible."

Gary walked to the corner of the room and clicked on his radio. The mumble of his conversation pulsated in the background.

My knees were stiff as I sat down on the nearby couch. I wiped my damp hand on my dress and stared at James, who bounced Roberta next to me. He was fixated on her, probably lost in thought.

"James," I whispered. "How will we ever get to safety? We've become an island in a terrible storm."

He flatted the smile he'd held for Roberta and looked at me deeply, as though into my very soul. He swallowed hard. "One step at a time. We'll be okay." He lightened his voice at the end of his blanket statement of assurance.

The words *okay* washed over me but didn't bring me peace.

"I don't see how you can say that." I shuddered and looked around the room.

Was there anything we could float on? How long did we have before the building crumbled beneath us? Brooke squirmed in my arms to get down, and I clenched her closer to me. I couldn't let her go.

"I'll do everything I can to get you and the girls to safety," James said as he put his arm around my shoulder and pulled me in close. Brooke wrestled against my tight grip and cried out.

"Let her go, Sharon," James said. "She's fine. We're fine."

I didn't believe him. How could we all be okay when the waters rose, threatening to engulf us?

"All right," Gary shouted out from across the room and walked toward us. "There's a riverboat coming, and we'll be able to have the women and children leave from the front door. They're taking people to the university. It's on higher ground. James, you and I can work to salvage items from the first floor while we wait for our turn."

I clasped James' shirt. "I can't go without you!" I stammered.

James lifted Brooke off my lap and set her down. She stopped crying. He put his hands on my shoulders and turned me toward himself. "Sharon." He pulled me into his chest and whispered in my ears. "Be strong for the girls. You can do it."

Pushing back against his embrace, I implored him with my eyes. "James, how can you be so strong? Where? Where's your help coming from?"

James' lips parted, and he took in a deep breath. "I'm praying, Sharon. Just like my mom taught me to. I'm praying real hard."

I closed my eyes and tried to picture myself kneeling down beside my bed as I'd done as a small girl. Nope, I couldn't do it.

Chapter 19

Opening my eyes, I pursed my lips and spoke to James. "I don't see what good it will do. Why didn't God just stop the rain before it ever came to this? Now we have our babies to worry about, not just us." Tears welled in my eyes, then poured out. I gasped and placed my hand over my mouth.

"I don't know why. But you don't have a choice in what has to be done. You have to go alone with the girls. You do have a choice in how you handle it. You can choose to let fear grip you, or you can find resolve to face things as best you can." James pulled me to him, gave me a squeezing hug and then planted a kiss on my lips. "I'll see you as soon as I can. I love you, sweets." He kissed Roberta, who'd wiggled off the couch and sat at his feet. Then he picked up Brooke a few feet away, swung her in the air, and gave her a peck on the cheek. "You girls be good for Mom." Then he walked over to Gary.

I sat staring at Brooke and Roberta, who played, oblivious to the surrounding chaos. Swallowing back the tears, I clenched my teeth and focused on breathing through my nose. It was up to fate and chance now. A chance that we'd make it out of the crumbling building and to safety.

CHAPTER 20

I PACED THE SMALL DORM ROOM, FLITTING MY GAZE from where the girls slept on a small cot to the walls and then the window. *The sterile student housing was safe.* I'd used the sentence as a mantra to reassure myself and calm my nerves for what felt like forever.

Fear had pulsated through my body earlier as I watched families pouring into the facility, and James still hadn't joined us. The girls needed to sleep, so I'd pushed past my resolve to stand there waiting for him and had taken an offer for a room from one of the volunteers.

As I walked to the window, I grasped my paper coffee cup and sipped the lukewarm drink. *When would James arrive?* It had already been a few hours.

From the main-floor window, I could see volunteers out in the rain, pointing some people to student housing and redirecting others. Surely, he'd be told where to find the girls and me.

I shook my head at the memory of the boat ride to the university. I'd clung to the girls the best that I could as I struggled to manage them. Feeling faint from holding my breath, I'd

Chapter 20

focused on the inside of the boat, not taking in the scene of disaster in surrounding me.

"Thank God that's over," I stated out loud.

God?

I turned and walked back over to the door to set more pacing in motion. "Yes, God, where are you? Are you here in the flood?" Tiptoeing past the girls, I saw their calm faces while they slept. They were at peace. "I want that," I whispered. "I want absolute peace, no matter what."

God?

Silence answered my question, and I turned to walk back to the window.

The door rattled, and I jumped and spun in place to see James peeking through the small slit in the doorway. "James," I declared.

He opened the door and walked in. I ran and threw my arms around him, clinging to his neck.

"Sweets," he whispered and kissed my ear. "I'm here. We're okay."

"I was so worried about you," I murmured into his chest. "How'd you find us? I've been watching...I...oh, James." Tears poured onto his shoulder.

We clung to one another, with James rocking me back and forth.

"You're lucky you had a ride in a riverboat from the front step. They afforded Gary and me the pleasure of being rescued from the roof."

I gasped. "No!"

"Shoot, I shouldn't have told you." He pulled away and wiped the tears from my eyes with his fingertips, then leaned in to kiss my cheek. "Everyone is safe."

"Yes, thankfully."

"I'm going to help serve some food. They've been able to

rescue some supplies from nearby stores, but for now, we have some MREs to hand out."

I furrowed my brow. "M...R...E? What is that? Some kind of fruit?"

James laughed out loud. "No." He shook his head and smiled. "It's an acronym for Meal, Ready-to-Eat. They're from the military."

I scrunched my nose. "What in the world?"

"Actually, they're pretty great. You'll be surprised." He went over to the cot and knelt beside the girls, who'd slept through the commotion. "Our sleeping angels."

I walked behind him and watched his face as he beamed at them.

"Yes, sleeping," I agreed.

James stood up and grabbed my hand. "I'll see you down there when they get up. If I don't, I'll bring some MREs back with me."

"Okay."

"Lie down with them and get some rest. We're together now. Let the peace of knowing we're safe lull you to sleep."

"Hmm, I'll try, James."

He kissed me again and opened the door with the grace of a surgeon performing surgery.

Let peace lull me?

I inched over to the other cot on the side of the room, lay down, and covered up with the provided rough woolen blanket. I curled up in the bed and watched my girls lying still. Did God see the fear that had bathed my day?

I sighed. *Let it go, Sharon. Get some sleep.* Once I reassured myself, I let exhaustion take over.

❄

Chapter 20

When I woke up the next morning, James was next to me on the small cot, and I could hear his rhythmic breathing. Clueless as to how much time had passed, I determined to lie still.

Remorse from my selfish response yesterday knotted my stomach. I'd rooted myself in fear, whereas James had risked his life for mine, and now, here we were, safely together. Why had doubt risen to the surface in the eye of my storm?

I turned my shoulder toward the noise of the girls stirring. Alarmed they may fall off the unfamiliar cot, I sat up and inched toward them.

Brooke sat up on the bed, rubbing and blinking her eyes. I waved to her and smiled, and she beamed.

"Hi, honey!" I whispered as I got up and moved over to her.

"Hi," James said groggily as he sat up.

"I'm sorry," I answered as I picked Brooke up. "I didn't mean to wake you up."

James sat and stretched. "Oh, I feel much better. How's my girl?" He reached for Brooke and took her in his arms. "You and the girls were fast asleep when I came back, so I took your MREs back. There are some other snacks in the corner."

Roberta stirred, and I sat down on the girls' cot.

"Look at us, all safe together," James said as he bounced Brooke on his knee. "Hard to believe we're here during the flood of the century."

Roberta crawled over the bed to me and laid her head on my lap. I rubbed her soft brown hair. "Really, James? It's that bad?"

"Let's put it this way, there should have been an ark to carry us to safety. It's colossal."

Brooke tried to wiggle out of his hands, and he set her on the floor. She walked around the room to explore the space.

"I see you have the diapers from the apartment," he continued. "Why don't we change the girls and head to the main room? I'd like to see how I can help."

James had a servant's heart. He spied out needs and volunteered to offer aid. I admired his resilience, and him.

"You just never stop, do you?" I walked over to where he was and sat on his lap. "You put others first, and you do it so well."

He touched my cheek and then brushed a wandering strand of hair and put it behind my ear. "I'm flattered you see it that way. Truly, though…it's you I think of first. Always you. I'm so thankful yesterday is over. Let's take on today together. Okay?"

My anchor, James, had weathered the storm like a diligent soldier, faithful to the task. I had drifted. "Okay, together." I tilted my face down and kissed him.

"Whoop!" James bellowed.

CHAPTER 21

IN THE UNIVERSITY CAFETERIA, I SAT WITH THE GIRLS while they finished eating an assortment of food given to those of us living in the dorms. The hodgepodge menu was received with gratitude by both the girls and me. Roberta chased the peas on her plate with a spoon, while Brooke had long since tossed her spoon and used her hands to scoop the instant potatoes into her mouth instead.

It had been a week since the flood, and we'd gotten word to our families that we were safe. James kept busy helping serve food, while I managed the girls. The US Army Corps would soon determine when residents could return to their homes, and how help would be provided to dehumidify buildings, if possible, before the cold weather set in.

I finished up my chili and pushed my bowl away, then watched Brooke and Roberta enjoy their meal. "Okay, girls, finish up your supper, then we're going to find Daddy." I scanned the room for any sign of James, who had left earlier for a school board meeting.

"There's my girls!" I heard James say from behind me. "Mmm, your supper looks good, Brooke," he teased. "Yum." He sat down next to me.

"Hey, there," I said as I inched closer to him.

"Hey yourself, sweets."

"Any news about our situation?" I reached for a napkin from the table and wiped my hands.

"Yup, they announced all teacher contracts are on hold for the time being. That's the job status. At the meeting, Brad invited us to come and stay with them in North Pole temporarily until we figure out where the teaching jobs will be. So?"

I nodded, and a smile grew across my face. "That would be wonderful. We could get away from the chaos. It's very kind of them."

"Phew, I'm glad you think so. Didn't know if you'd be up for it or not. It's out of town, so you'd be housebound. Ha, what am I talking about? I'd be housebound too, come to think of it." James helped Roberta put some peas on her spoon. "I'll tell Brad we're in. He said he can come get us tonight."

An opportunity to leave the communal living space was a welcome change. Gratitude rose in my heart, and I took in a cleansing breath. "I'm game. I'll clean the girls up, and we can be ready."

James took a napkin off the table and wiped Brooke's fingers. "Wow, she made a fun mess." He cleared his throat. "We'll need to talk later, about a new teaching job."

I narrowed my eyes and searched James' face. "What do you mean?"

"The school district here doesn't anticipate needing as many teachers. Folks are displaced. They're encouraging us to look for other jobs, which could be anywhere in Alaska. Brad has some leads to share.

Here we go again.

I felt cautiously optimistic. A new beginning seemed intriguing after the bumpy start here. "Sounds interesting," I stated and stood up.

"Sharon? It means moving," he said, looking up at me. He then rose to face me.

"I know," I answered, believing I could start over somewhere new.

"It could mean moving even farther away than here."

"Aren't you the one who says, 'one step at a time'?" I gave James a playful wink and bent over to pick peas up off the floor.

"Yes, yes, I do. I'll go call Gary and be right back."

I continued to tidy our area. A move to North Pole and then the unknown. Another adventure was underway. Our only obstacle was our own resolve.

I JUGGLED THE GIRLS BETWEEN MYSELF AND JAMES AS we sat in the small mail plane taking us from Galena, Alaska, to Bethel. Curiously, the flight service hauled passengers along with US Postal Service bags and boxes to rural Alaskan villages.

Our plane had stopped at two other small villages along the Yukon, and now we followed the Kuskokwim River south. The land below us was spotted with small lakes and ponds and a wide greenbelt along a main river.

James tapped me on the shoulder, and I turned from the window.

"I asked the lady at the reservation desk if there was a meal served," he said.

I laughed and shook my head.

"Hey, she didn't laugh; she just looked at me funny and said no."

I repositioned Brooke on my lap, as she'd slumped over into a nap and laid her head on my shoulder. "I wouldn't trade a meal for our trip in a small plane. Jump seats with luggage in front of us for a footrest." I pointed to the pile strapped down close to our seats. "Doesn't get better than this."

"I'm glad you're up for it, sweets. When we rolled into Tok last year, I was a little disappointed. I was hoping for more of an Alaskan experience outside the city. Something drastically different than what we knew."

"Oh, so we can all blame the mighty flood on your desire for a transplant?"

James looked up from the book he held open for Roberta, who sat on his lap. "Whoa, there. Not quite. Jumping into the school year in October will have its own challenges as well." He reached into a bag beside him and retrieved the small, silky blanket Roberta loved to have with her when she napped. "You know what?

"Hmm?"

"When we rolled a six and landed in Alaska, this is the kind of life I had hoped for."

"You've got your wish, James. I'm glad there's a little job for me at the school too. I'm excited about helping with the deaf class and having someone to watch the girls." Catching myself in a yawn, I continued. "Sounds like Bethel is a friendly place."

James yawned too, then exclaimed, "Stop it, now I'm getting sleepy."

"Take a nap." I repositioned my head against the seat and closed my eyes. "I'm going to try to." In my mind's eye, I saw the western village of Bethel as remote and quaint, with Eskimos wearing parkas waiting to greet us with wide smiles. Uncertain of my stereotypical imaginings, and unsure of what things would really be like, I thought instead about what I wanted to gain from the experience. I hoped for a grand purpose in our time with the children. Would I have much to contribute? Was I chalking up chances to make an impact? Was I making assumptions?

The certainty behind our decision to go to Bethel propelled me enthusiastically forward. Joining James in the classroom and embracing new experiences sounded like the right balance of necessity and fun—just like a mail plane packed with packages and passengers.

As we began our decent, snowflakes swirled to the ground. When we arrived and ambled out of the small plane, arctic winds blew at our faces, stinging my cheeks. Narrowing my eyes to keep out the cold, I didn't take the time to look around. I was busy sheltering Brooke with my arms and her blanket, which I struggled to keep wrapped around her.

The superintendent from the school district drove us to our cabin near the school and helped shuffle in our belongings. He introduced himself as Howard and unlocked the door to the small cabin. He tipped his hat to me and shook James' hand. "Make yourselves comfortable. I've another commitment to go to. I'll see you tomorrow," he stated, then left us to explore our new home.

James shut the door and leaned against it, letting out a sigh. "He seems nice. Wow, what a fierce wind. Thank God it didn't blow real hard until after the plane landed. At least we don't have to go back out again today."

I set Brooke down and let her walk around the one-room cabin. "James, this is going to be very cozy."

The house wasn't a log cabin as I'd imagined, but a small house with less than one thousand square feet. We'd entered from an oversized entryway with hooks along the wall for our coats. Ahead of us was a small galley kitchen with pot and pans hanging from the roof. To the left was a living room with a stove tucked into the corner near the door we'd walked through and some furniture. A pile of wood was neatly stacked next to the woodstove, and a pair of gloves sat atop it. In the living room were two doors; one was open, and the other shut.

I moved to the open door and saw a bed and dresser in the room.

James walked over near the kitchen, where a large fifty-gallon barrel was placed on a wooden stand. "Howard said it's our water."

"Water?" I questioned, walking over to where he stood.

"Yup, they'll come and fill it from a pumper truck. Not many folks having running water here."

I smoothed my turtleneck sweater-top and placed my hands on my hips. "Then I'm even more grateful to be at the school during the day." Moving to the back toward the living room, I reached for the handle of the other door in the cabin. "Where's the bathroom?"

James picked up Roberta and swung her in the air, and she squealed. "I'm so glad we agreed to come before we knew about our living conditions." He placed Roberta down and reached for Brooke.

"What? Why?" I began to feel like I was going to burn up with my coat still on.

"There isn't one."

I pushed on a wooden door. "No bathroom? What's in here?" Certain he was mistaken, I unlatched the door and stepped into a small room with a slanted roof. The stale smell of damp wood ticked my nostrils. Two five-gallon buckets stood in a corner, and I saw a roll of toilet paper on the floor. "James?" I called out.

"Honey, It's the honey bucket room," James announced with enthusiasm. "I remember my mom telling me about the one she had as a girl in North Dakota..." His voice trailed off, and he clasped his mouth with his hand as he looked at me.

"It's not the nineteenth century anymore. Is this for real? What about the girls' diapers? What will we do with those? And what about washing our hands? I've read Little House on Prairie and imagined the hardships they endured, but I never pictured myself using a hand washing station and—"

James wrapped me in a hug while the girls played chase. "Sweets, we've signed up for a grand adventure. Remember, one day at a time. We'll find a way to make it wonderful." He held my hands and took a step back. "I'll be the chief diaper-washing guy. We'll get a bucket and let them soak. Um, yeah, they'll probably freeze in the room since it's not heated. But I promise you won't have to deal with it. We can take showers at school, and they provide two meals a day for the kids, and we'll eat with them."

I lifted my gaze from my feet to search his dark brown eyes. Although the cabin and living space would be a challenge, James' love for us and his devotion to the girls and me was obvious. "Okay, I promise to take it one day at a time."

The promise to measure out patience would not be the hardest task of each day. Reminding myself of the fact that I was a devoted mom who'd committed to being strong and genuine for my girls was the enduring balance that I'd claimed almost two years ago to the day.

"James," I said, too loudly. "The girls."

He stood staring at me and shook his head. "What?"

"It's their birthday," I stammered. "Tomorrow!" I kneeled down and received a hug from Roberta, and she patted my shoulder. Her almost-two-year-old ways of mimicking us was a reminder to be mindful of what I modeled. "I was going to make a cake and wrap up the dresses my parents gave them. Oh James." Tears welled up in my eyes and I turned my head away so Roberta wouldn't see the sadness on my face. "I forgot."

"They don't know any different, sweets. We'll have a party. Leave it to me."

I nodded and sat down at the nearby table. How had I let it slip? How had I let the move impede celebrating our girls?

I looked out the window, noting the similarity of the area and the prairie landscape of Ohio. Perhaps the flat tundra was something I could identify with. The low bushes and ground cover had turned a rusty color, signaling the end of one season and the ushering in of another. Could I relate to the change of season and resolve to make it better in the next one? Where could I turn to draw strength? I closed my eyes, shutting out the giggles and antics between James and the girls.

God? Maybe? Can You help?

I'd set prayer aside for some time now, and somehow, from deep within me, this prayer had risen to the surface.

CHAPTER 22

I PUSHED IN THE SMALL CHAIRS NEXT TO THE ROUND table in the classroom, then kneeled to pick up the remnants of paper from the Thanksgiving craft we'd done earlier in the afternoon that now littered the floor. Working alongside another lady and helping a deaf student in the latter part of the school day was gratifying. I appreciated the opportunity to make an impact in children's lives.

As I placed the trash in the garbage, I noticed the superintendent's wife step into the room. "Hi, Marsha," I said.

"Hi, Sharon. The boys and I stopped by to say hi to Howard. I decided while they played with his typewriter, I'd visit with you. How are you enjoying life in the bush?" She placed her purse on the table and set down her coat with a fur ruff.

"Bush?" I looked over my shoulder as though gazing out the window briefly.

Marsha chuckled. "I guess you haven't heard that Alaskan saying just yet. The bush is any part of Alaska not connected to the road system."

I'd heard it before in passing but hadn't connected it to my own situation.

"I see. We're doing well. The girls love spending time with

Anna while I'm here at the school. Do you know her? She's a local Eskimo woman who has a couple of grown kids, but she loves the little ones. She's watched a few other kids in the past, I guess. Brooke and Roberta come home exhausted from their playtimes, as we call them."

"I do know Anna. She's a kind soul. Yesterday, I saw them all playing out in the snow. Did she make the cute kuspuks the girls had on?"

"Yes, aren't they precious?" The hooded overshirt with large pockets had become a clothing item the girls loved to put on over their coats and wear to Anna's.

"I find little treasures in their pockets all the time. You know two-year-olds, they are always picking up the strangest things and putting them in handy spots and then forgetting all about them. Cracker pieces, crayons, and so on. So, how long have you lived here?"

"We've been here a few years. But, next year, we're leaving the bush. Howard has accepted a position in Glennallen. So, we'll be on the road system." Marsha folded her hands and closed her eyes. "Thank you, Jesus. I'm ready to settle down, buy some land, and stay put for a while." She picked up her coat. "Do you and James have plans for Thanksgiving?"

"No, we don't."

With only two weeks left in November, the holiday was quickly approaching.

"Well, now you do. We'd like you to join us at our place. No need to bring anything. I've divided the menu with a couple of other ladies already. Being in the bush means ordering food months ahead of time. We've had side dishes ready and in the freezer for weeks now."

"Wow, thanks."

James peeked his head in. "Sweets? I'll be ready to go after I'm done with diapers." He was gone as fast as he'd arrived.

"Diapers?" Marsha questioned.

"Um, yeah. James launders the girls' cloth diapers. He thaws them in the boiler room, washes them out, and brings them home." I shook my head. "I wasn't ready for the dry cabin part of our adventure."

"He deserves a medal!" Marsha stated. "I didn't realize you were staying over there. Perhaps because you arrived partway into the new school year." She leaned over closer to me. "Keep your head up though. I heard there is another place opening up, and it will be much better."

"Oh?" I asked. "I haven't heard of it."

"I probably shouldn't have said anything. That's Howard's job, not mine. I'll write the four of you down for Thanksgiving dinner then." Marsha moved over to the door. "Would you like to come over Wednesday and help me make the pies? It's nice to have those fresh."

"Sure. Sounds great. James wants to take the girls to see a dogsled team. I don't mind missing out for some baking."

"Can you come around two? Does that work?"

"Yes, thanks."

"See you."

As Marsha stepped out of the room, I felt a sense of belonging rise within me. We'd grown use to our evenings in a small cabin without running water, and we were warmly welcomed into the community. With Thanksgiving approaching, I could affirm there was much to be grateful for.

WHEN I WALKED INTO THE ARCTIC ENTRY OF HOWARD and Marsha's home, I could hear the family talking in unison. I put my ear to the door, straining to make out what was being said. I didn't want to interrupt something important.

"To You O my strength, I will sing praises;

"For God is my defense,

"My God of mercy."

Howard's voice carried over the others. "Well done boys. You've memorized all the way to verse seventeen now."

When he stopped speaking, I knocked on the door to announce my presence.

"Coming," Marsha called out, and I heard footsteps approaching the door. Her bright smile greeted me, and she held the door open for me. "Hi, Sharon. C'mon in."

Howard stood up from the couch, closed a large book, and placed it on the coffee table in front of him. "Hi, Sharon. We'll leave you ladies to your baking. The boys and I are going to watch the dog sledding with James and the girls."

As he finished speaking, their two boys jumped up and down.

"Thanks, Daddy!" their oldest shouted out, and the boys scrambled to grab coats off some hooks next to where I stood.

Marsha's smile widened. "You guys have a great time." She leaned toward Howard and gave him a kiss, then waved me over to the kitchen.

"How's your crew today?" she asked.

"Good." I shook my head. "My girls are growing up so fast. They are talking so much these days. They get frustrated when *we* don't understand *them*." I followed Marsha to her kitchen, where she had some baking supplies on the counter.

"These are such impressionable years. We only get them for such a short time. Train them up in the way they should go. You know how it goes." She looked at me as though I'd followed what she'd said, but I hadn't.

"Not sure I've heard the saying? Is it Alaskan?" I asked as I put on an apron that I'd brought with me.

She placed a hand on her forehead. "There I go again, rambling. Not Alaskan. It's a Bible verse." Her kind smile brightened her green eyes, which matched the apron she had already tied on. The floral print was bright and cheery, with green leaves accentuating the blossoms. "There is a verse from the book of Proverbs in the Bible, and it encourages us as parents to teach our children according to God's ways. Then when our kids are older, they have those truths they've learned to fall back on."

I cleared my throat, feeling a surge of guilt for overhearing their family time before I knocked on their door.

"Were you practicing verses before I came in?" I stammered. "I heard you all talking and paused before I knocked."

Marsha pulled a bag of flour off a shelf and placed it on the counter next to a bowl. "Don't feel bad. We were practicing our memory verses together."

"Memory?" I asked.

"Yes, our church is having a special Thanksgiving service on Friday evening, and we will recite some verses together as a family." She laughed. "We let the boys pick the verses, and I'm not sure why they picked the ones they did. They weren't so much about Thanksgiving. Maybe they're verses they've heard us recite when they're afraid at night."

Narrowing my eyes, I searched hers. They memorized Bible verses? I'd been to a church growing up—we recited some written prayers and sang hymns—but we never committed scriptures to memory. "I see," I said, not sure what else to say.

She moved to the sink and washed her hands, drying them on her apron. "What kind of pie do you want to make first? Apple or pumpkin?"

"How about..." I followed her example and washed my hands at the sink. "Apple. And I'll peel them. I love seeing how long of a peeling string I can make."

"Hey, I like doing that too! We have a lot in common."

A lot in common? Her comment confused me. She had three boys and I had two girls. She was almost six feet, and I was under five feet. I began peeling an apple while my mind searched for common ground.

"I see your wheels are turning. Did I say something

confusing about the Bible?" Marsha commented as she took her small, paring knife and began slicing the apple I'd just peeled.

"Well, I have to admit, I'm not familiar with the church and Bible learning you're talking about."

"And I have to admit, I go on and on making assumptions instead of asking questions." She set down the peeler and tilted her head to the side. "I grew up knowing about a personal relationship with Jesus. I talk and talk like I would with Howard. I should be more sensitive to the fact that not everyone has had the same experience. Would you and your family like to come to our little church on Friday for the short Thanksgiving service?"

"I'll check with James and see if he has any other plans."

"It's nothing fancy. We dress casual. Wear what's warm. It won't be a long service, and we'll have some snacks here after." Marsha moved to the stove and turned it on. "What will your family back home be doing for Thanksgiving?"

An excellent question. I'd been so busy getting settled in Bethel and adjusting to the transition of working part time, I hadn't been in as much contact with our extended family as I should have.

"I'm not sure. Probably gathering at my mom's place. James' family has a big family meal at his grandma's place in North Dakota."

It was times like this when the distance from family weighed down on me. In bringing the girls to Alaska, we'd removed them from the experiences like James had had with his grandparents. What kind of legacy were we passing on to our girls?

Marsha carried herself with confidence. She'd had a different upbringing than mine. I was curious if that was what made her shine.

"I'm looking forward to having your sweet family here with us tomorrow," she said as she sprinkled some sugar on the apples in a bowl between us.

Chapter 22

"Thanks for having us. I wasn't sure what we were going to do. We've been displaced since the flood."

We heard stomping in the entryway, and Marsha stepped out of the kitchen. "Okay." I heard her say, then she appeared back at my side. "Leave the pie for now. We have a quick errand to run," Marsha stated.

"Oh." I untied my apron and set it on the counter near the sink.

Assuming we needed something from the store, I bundled up in my winter coat and followed Marsha outside to her truck, then hopped in the passenger seat.

Marsha hummed to herself while we drove the short distance between her house and a home near the school. The gray bungalow was within walking distance of the school, and I'd already noticed it on my walks. I'd been told the sturdy-looking structure was used for out-of-town students who came to the Bethel area.

"Can you give me a hand?" Marsha asked. "I have a couple of things I need to get from here for tomorrow." She exited the truck before I could answer.

"Sure," I said as I followed her down the swept sidewalk.

I wonder why it's cleared of snow.

Marsha and I stomped the snow off our boots and walked into the duplex.

"Surprise!" shouted James, Howard, and Howard's
boys.

Brooke and Roberta clapped.

Inside the bungalow were our few household items. "What?" I said, astounded and confused.

"Welcome home, sweets," James said as he walked over and gave me a kiss.

"Really?" My heart pounded. "We get to live *here*?" I'd heard it had running water, three bedrooms, and good insulation. I never knew us living here was a possibility.

"Yes," Howard announced. "I have to apologize for not thinking of it earlier. We have two more boys coming from upriver, and they will need a place to stay. One will be in James' class and the other in your deaf class. In exchange for the housing, you'll be their dorm parents. Is that agreeable?"

I nodded before I spoke. "Most definitely. Thank you so much."

Roberta walked over and swung her arm around my leg, and I looked at all the smiling faces of the friends who'd gone out of their way to help us.

Marsha walked over and gave me a hug. "The pie-making was a little trick to have you out of the house. I hope you don't mind."

"No, I don't," I said. I returned the smiles, beaming from the depths of my core. Our rural adventure had turned out to be a wonderful chance to make friends with kind people.

"Well, thank God we get to bless you for Thanksgiving," Marsha said. "Earlier, I put some food in the fridge for you—and some treats for the girls. Okay crew, on three," she said, then in unison, she and her family shouted out, "Welcome home!"

Welcome home, indeed. The only missing ingredient was finding out what Marsha had that I didn't. What drove her to display such kindness? What lit up her face and mannerisms? I felt like James and I were both agreeable people who cared for others, but something was different about Howard and Marsha. We were taking steps forward as family, but I sensed there was more for us to learn. Maybe we could learn it from them.

CHAPTER 23

On Thanksgiving Day, we slept in as best we could with the twins jabbering together in their bed, which was right next to ours. Their giggles were contagious, and their perspectives on life were endearing. They found silliness and joy in the smallest of things, and it bubbled over onto us. Soon, we were laughing at their laughter.

I rolled over and cuddled with James "Happy Thanksgiving," I said and gave him a light kiss on his cheek.

"Hm, thank *you*," he answered. "Now, tell me, Mrs. Kline. What are you thankful for today?"

Roberta and Brooke must have heard our hushed voices, as they squirmed out of their bed and came over to ours. They tried to climb in with us, and I sat up and pulled them onto our bed one at a time.

"I'm thankful for my family." I brushed Brooke's hair away from her eyes. "I never could have imagined our Alaskan life together. I'm also thankful for new friends along the way." I propped my pillow behind my back. The girls wiggled their way under the covers and tried to tickle James' neck like he did theirs.

After breakfast, I cleaned off the table and set out construction paper to make a Thanksgiving craft with the girls. Marsha's words about raising children in a pattern had resonated with me, and I was determined to start more traditions with Brooke and Roberta. "James, will you please pass me those crayons next to the calculator?"

"Sure."

I took a crayon from the jar, then I placed Brooke's small hand flat on the paper and began tracing around it with the crayon. She giggled as the crayon moved between her fingers.

"Tickle, Mommy," she said, and threw her head back in laughter.

"Sorry, honey. Let's trace your other hand. We're going to make something pretty for the window."

The girls cooperated with my simple instructions and let me trace their hands, but soon they were in middle of the room, dancing with Daddy. It had been their morning routine for quite some time now. I supposed he'd started his own traditions with them long ago.

I stayed at the table and wrote the names of family and friends on each paper finger. I cut them out and taped them together to make them look like turkey feathers. Proud of my efforts, I held them up to catch some of the light from over the table. "There," I stated.

The word fell on deaf ears, as James and the girls were lost in their laughter. I smiled at the scene of the girls clapping and kicking their feet and attempting to jump up and down without stumbling.

I walked to the window and taped the makeshift turkeys to it as our reminder to be thankful. Would this simple paper-made image help me in my times of doubt? Would the girls grow up to be thankful? Or would they stumble? I had certainly fallen flat on my face more than once while they watched nearby.

I rubbed my forearms and turned to the scene in the living room. The girls' hair was all sweaty as they began to wrestle their daddy and ride him like a horse. Their imaginations were blossoming, and their daddy was happy to play along, adding his part to the way they would view the world.

THE SNOW CRUNCHED UNDER OUR BOOTS AS WE walked to Howard and Marsha's that afternoon. Brooke and Roberta watched their feet as they shuffled between James and me.

"I love the smell of woodsmoke when we go outside for a walk. It's cozy," James said and raised his chin, taking in a deep breath.

"Cozy and cold. When the snow crackles underfoot as loud as it does now, it means it's awfully chilly out here," I responded.

"I'm sorry, I couldn't hear you. I was too busy smelling." He laughed. "Sometimes, it's best not to think of how cold it is and let your mind wander to the good things that are only possible because it's so cold. Me, I'm thankful for the frozen river, so we can travel for basketball games soon and—"

"Frozen river?" I questioned.

"During basketball season, we'll drive the vans on the Kuskokwim River to get from one village to the next," he said casually.

"Oh my. Now that sounds unbelievably, bitterly cold. And scary."

"Like I said, I don't put too much thought into it. It's the way it is, and if the river didn't freeze, we couldn't travel this time of year."

"I suppose you're right, but wow."

As we entered their arctic entrance. I was thankful for a warm house to visit in and that we didn't have to travel on a frozen river to get there. I picked up Brooke, James picked up Roberta, and we knocked on the door.

"Heh-whoa?" Brooke called out, trying to say hello.

We laughed as the door opened and Marsha waved us in.

"Come in, come in. Brr, it's cold out there," Marsha said as she held the door for us.

A couple of other families were there already. The kids were playing a game at the coffee table in the living room, and the adults were standing in the kitchen, which was open to the dining area next to the living room. Marsha helped undress the girls from their layers of warm gear: coats, sweaters, scarves, hats and mittens. Then she helped pull off their boots.

"I'd forgotten how much work it is to get a little one all bundled up." She pulled off Brooke's hat and the static from the dry air made Brooke's hair stand it on end. Long ago, I'd given up on styling the girls' hair during the winter and now simply used barrettes to pull it back from their eyes. Brooke had pink and Roberta had purple. The simple items helped distinguish them from each other too. "All right, now that we have you cuties out of your coats, would you like to come here and see the kids?" Marsha kneeled down and offered her hand for either of them to take.

Brooke reached out and took her hand while she looked at me for reassurance. Roberta followed her to the living room, and I stepped closer to the kitchen table.

James introduced me to another couple he knew from school, and then a young man came over and told us his name and how'd he'd come to work in the area with a missions organization.

Marsha brought me cup of coffee, and we visited at the table.

"Ah, it's so good to sit down. We'll wait on one more family, then we'll be ready to eat. How's your day been?" she asked.

"We had a quiet morning. I did a small craft with the girls but they're still little. You know how short attention spans are at their age. We'll have to wait for them to be older to build more traditions together." I wrapped my hands around my mug, stealing its warmth.

"Oh boy, yes. Those were fun times, but I must admit, I'm enjoying my boys at this stage too. Each season has its own challenges and its own blessings. The trick is learning to appreciate the blessings. They can be disguised."

Feet stomped on the front steps, and Marsha got up to open the door. Another family walked in and settled in among the group.

After introductions, Howard gave a quick whistle. "Let's pray, folks, and thank God for all this food. We'll make a big circle and hold hands."

We all stood and joined hands, encircling both the coffee table and oversized kitchen table. Howard led the prayer.

"Dear Lord, thank you for the day we have set aside to recognize that You are the giver all things. We thank you for the food we are about to share and the friends we'll share it with. Thank you most of all for Your son, Jesus, and the gift that He is to us. Amen."

Amens came from around the room, and I looked up at James, who stood next to me. He gave me a wink and squeezed my hand.

Marsha clapped. "Oh, I almost forgot, we have a little something to share before the meal. Come on boys." She motioned for her boys to join her and held out her arms. Together, they sang a song of thanksgiving and did the corresponding sign language motions. I was impressed with the work that had gone into the special selection, and noted that I could ask Marsha for help practicing the sign language that I might need to communicate with the deaf child coming to live with us.

After dinner, we played games and visited while the kids ran back and forth between the back bedroom, the hall, and the kitchen table.

One of the other families had a teenage daughter, Miah, who had latched onto my girls. Brooke and Roberta were mesmerized by her, following her around and wanting to sit on her lap. I could see her natural way and her kind smile as she read books to them and attempted to color with them at the table.

"Mrs. Kline?" Miah called from the table. "Can I show you something I taught the girls?"

"Sure." I got up and walked to where they were.

"Okay, let's show your mom and dad."

"Okay, Miah," Brooke answered, saying Miah's name clearly.

Miah began to sing a song, and my girls joined in. I sat in awe at how quickly they'd learned it. It was a counting song that numbered the ways God loved them. A tear formed in my eye. Miah had captured their hearts, and she cared enough to teach my girls a song about the everlasting love of God. The girls watched their fingers as they tried to keep up with the simple counting in the song, and they looked to James and me with delighted smiles.

CHAPTER 24

I couldn't get the image out of my mind of Brooke and Roberta enjoying and singing about a God they didn't know. Perhaps they liked their new friend so much that they were attracted to the song and actions.

I had mentioned praying to the girls at times, but they didn't see an example in me. We weren't godless, but we weren't what I considered godly. We hadn't even been to church in Alaska before.

I didn't know what to expect from our visit. And I didn't know what made this church unique. But I knew it was, because Martha and her family were different than other church people I'd met.

As I stirred the pot of chili on the stove, I imagined us going as a family to the evening Thanksgiving service. We'd walk in, watch from a distance, and tell our new friends we'd consider coming back someday—to be polite.

"You ready, sweets?" James asked from the hall, where he buttoned up his sports coat.

"Oh, don't you look sharp," I said, walking closer to him.

"I always look this good. They call me Mr. Kline: tall, dark, and handsome." He raised his chin and formed a closed-lip smile, then gave me a wink.

"Miah, Miah," Roberta said as she ambled down the hall.

"Sounds like the girls enjoyed playing with Miah last night," James said as he picked Roberta up. "You ready for church?" he asked her. Then he spun her around and set her down.

I moved back to the kitchen and pulled the oven mitts out of the drawer. "I'll be ready in a minute. I need to pack up the chili first."

Marsha had invited us over after church to eat and play games, and I had offered to bring food.

James went to the hooks by the door, pulled down the girls' coats and bundled the girls up.

As I placed the pot by the door, I bit at my lip and watched the clock. "Guess we'd better hurry."

"Um?" James questioned as he worked to zip up Roberta's coat.

"We don't want to be late." I put Brooke's hat on and then fidgeted with my mittens, not wanting to wear them while I carried the pot.

"Just be cool. We're not late." James bent over and tied his boots. "At least not yet. Are you nervous about going to church?"

"Choich?" Brooke said and looked up at me. "Mommy, choich."

"Yes, church, honey," I said to Brooke and tied her hat on. I inched toward the door and looked at James. "I'm not so sure about church since I haven't been in years."

James reached out and opened the door. "Good news is, it's not a big place. We'll probably know everyone. We can visit with friends and then go over to Howard and Marsha's."

After the short drive, we entered the small church. People stood visiting in a large foyer, which had a coat rack and small table with Thanksgiving decorations on it. The space was invit-

Chapter 24

ing, but I wondered if I could find some water before we settled in. My mouth was dry.

The girls let out a squeal, and I scanned the room to see what had caught their attention while I still tried to help them take off their hats and mittens. I spotted Anna, the woman who watched the girls during the school week while I worked at the school. She waved at us and walked over.

"Hi," I said.

Brooke tugged away from me to reach out to Anna

"Hello!" Anna said with excitement. She turned to the girls. "Hi, My-ah."

"Miah?" I looked around expecting to see the young girl from yesterday.

"Oh, I'm sorry." Anna touched my arm. "That's my name for your daughters. It means 'mine.' They're my *little* ones," she said and squatted next to them. It's such a treat watching your girls." She helped hang up the girls' things and took Roberta's hand. "Do you all want to come sit with us?" she asked.

I hesitantly answered, "sure" and joined her in the larger room.

I searched for James, who stood talking with someone closer to the door. Waving at him, I motioned in the direction I was walking and followed Anna.

It had pricked my ears to hear someone call my girls their own. I knew she meant no harm, but Brooke and Roberta were mine.

Squinting my eyes from the bright lights of the room I pursed my lips and remembered that I'd wanted a drink before church. "Anna?" I asked as I set my purse on the floor next to the chair I'd claimed.

"Yes?" she answered, helping Roberta up into the chair next to her girls.

"Where could I find some water?" I asked, knowing they may or may not have running water.

Anna looked up at me and smiled. "Back in lobby by the bathroom."

"Thanks." I hurried. And tried to swallow. It was bad enough that we were guests in a church we didn't know anything about. Now, I was scrambling for a drink like I hadn't taken care of myself.

I found some cups and a pitcher of water and gulped down a couple of glasses, then headed back to where the girls were clapping next to Anna.

My stomach began to harden. *Maybe I drank the water too fast.* I put my hand on my belly as I sat down and gave Anna and the girls a quick smile.

Anna leaned over toward me. "Are your girls okay to sing?"

"Sure, they love singing," I answered.

Anna pointed up front. "No, up there."

I narrowed my eyes and turned my head, looking for James. "Um, what do you mean?" I questioned.

"I've taught them songs. They can sing with me."

Unsure of how to respond, I nodded and looked down at my feet and the puddle that was forming on the floor from my wet boots. James nudged me as he took a seat.

I leaned over and whispered to him. "Anna asked if the girls could join her with a song."

"Neat," he answered and put his arm around my shoulder. I sensed he was comfortable with their participation, and I rested against him.

Piano music started, and Howard went to the front of the church. He read a couple of things from his Bible about thanksgiving. While he read the words, I stole glances around me. There were many empty chairs. Perhaps on Sundays it was full?

From the corner of my eye, I also watched Brooke and Roberta cuddle up together and lean over closer to Anna and her older daughters. Anna put her arm around my girls and pulled them in closer. I suppose she'd had years of raising and caring for kids and felt comfortable treating other people's kids like her own.

Howard called his family forward, and Marsha and the boys walked up front. I eased into my chair and watched them closely, smiling at their happy faces. Together, they recited the verses I'd heard them saying when I'd stopped in to help Marsha with the pies. The boys spoke clearly and proudly. Our friends were doing well at ingraining their strong Christian values in their kids.

We all clapped when they finished, and Howard announced that Anna had a children's special to share. Brooke and Roberta followed Anna to where she stood on the stage along with a couple of other kids. Anna moved out in front of them and then counted to three.

The little voices sang in unison about the love of God and His blessings coming down like rain. Brooke and Roberta smiled wide. Roberta tilted her head to the side to look past Anna, and waved when she saw me. I didn't see the girls' mouths move, but they joined in the hand motions.

I had no clue they had been learning a song, nor could I have imagined the joy I'd see on their faces. They loved being up in front, brave and participating. They looked so mature. Where had my babies gone?

James whispered to me. "They're so cute. I didn't know they'd learned these songs."

I formed a smile and nodded. Neither had I. Did it matter that Anna had been teaching them about her faith? Not at all. What hurt was that someone else was teaching my girls things that should have been important to all of us. I didn't have the knowledge to fall back on to teach them myself. I didn't even know where to begin.

A twinge of nausea turned my stomach. I'd fallen into the pit of jealousy over an older woman who clearly loved my girls—someone I trusted to help take care of them while I worked at the school. I closed my eyes and took in a slow breath. I felt sick about my negative response to something so beautiful and wholesome.

We all clapped as the children finished and found their way back to their seats. Brooke ran over and sat with James, and Roberta came to me saying, "Mommy, I sing."

A tear had formed in my eye, and I brushed it away. "Yes, honey. You sing beautifully."

There was no doubt in my mind that I needed to be a part of teaching my girls and instilling in them important values like love, faith, and God.

Oh, God, show me where to start?

CHAPTER 25

After the short church service, we walked to Marsha and Howard's home and shared the chili I'd made. Once those dishes were cleared away, I sat on the couch with my arms crossed, replaying in my mind the Thanksgiving service and how my girls had played a big role in its success without me. It had been my desire all along, and especially yesterday, on Thanksgiving morning, to begin traditions with them. I needed to find ways to teach them and show them the values James and I had.

"Sharon? Would you like some coffee?" Marsha asked from the kitchen. I blinked, willing myself to step out of the sludge I'd let myself slip into.

"Yes, thanks." I stood up, stretched, and moved to the kitchen.

"Everything okay?" she asked as she poured my coffee into a large mug.

"I was thinking about the mini-concert. It was a surprise to me that the girls would join Anna." I sipped the coffee. "A good surprise. I didn't know she was teaching them Sunday school songs."

"Isn't that wonderful," Marsha stated, smiling at me.

Repositioning my stance, I leaned into the counter and nodded in agreement. It was good, but where did I fit into it? "I didn't grow up learning those songs."

"Oh, don't feel bad. Your girls will be able to teach you." Marsha turned and put the coffee pot back on the stove and picked up her oven mitts to pull a pan from the oven. She called out over her shoulder as she placed the pan on a nearby hot pad. "Dessert is ready. Mark, would you please get the ice cream from the porch on your way by?" she asked her oldest son as he'd run to the counter.

My girls would teach me? The thought didn't sit well with me. I swallowed back the lump in my throat. Sipping my coffee, I watched all the other kids gather around the table and my girls pile onto their daddy's lap. There were oohs and aahs over the dessert we were about eat.

I'd been trying to tell Marsha that I didn't know where to begin and I wanted to know more. How could I communicate that to her? Was she the one who could help me? It appeared her faith was a part of her everyday life, as though she'd worked to make that way.

Howard scooped the blueberry crisp. James got up to serve ice cream, and I moved to sit near the girls and help them eat the treat.

"Where'd you get the berries?" I asked, noticing the smaller berries were unlike the ones I'd bought at the store in Fairbanks.

"We pick blueberries here. They are lowbush berries and probably a little more tart than the ones you're use to from out of state. However, everything tastes better with vanilla ice cream." She held up her spoon with a wide grin.

There were many things I could learn from my new friend. Entertaining, baking, and maybe how to find out more about teaching my kids.

Chapter 25

"I can send some home with you tonight if you like. We won't be able to eat all ours up before we move in a couple of months."

I stopped eating my dessert and searched her face. "I thought you weren't moving until next year?"

"Right, next year, in January. The school district there doesn't have a superintendent this school year, and a principal is filling in. We told them the soonest we could come was the new year." She set down her spoon. "I'm sorry you thought I meant the next school year."

My spoon felt heavy in my hand as I finished my blueberry crisp. I forced a smile, but all I wanted was to be alone. Here I'd found a friend who was the kind of mother I wanted to pattern my parenting after, and now I'd needed to say goodbye and try to find my way in the dark.

"Would anyone like to put a puzzle together tonight?" Howard asked as he scraped his bowl clean.

A puzzle. Here was a familiar thought in my mind—from before when my brother visited and we'd searched for a missing piece all evening. Here, I was the missing piece in the beautiful picture on the box, and we were all searching for it. You can't shave off another piece of cardboard to make it fit. It requires the exact one to complete it. What would it take for me to fit into life's puzzle?

I nodded and swallowed a mouthful of ice cream. Maybe putting a puzzle together on Thanksgiving Break could be a simple thing that James and I could do to show the girls we valued our time with them.

JAMES AND I SLEPT IN THE NEXT MORNING AND snuggled in bed, talking about our future in Bethel. The news of

Howard and Marsha's departure had stirred ideas about what we should do next year.

"Howard was telling me about a young teacher they had here who worked his summers as a border agent for the Feds. They need patrol agents all across the state. It might be one more added adventure for us if we spend summers doing that, and then I teach again each fall."

I was numb to the idea of jumping around from place to place. All I wanted was to introduce my girls to predictable patterns and a solid foundation. Could we provide them with stability even if we moved around?

"I don't know. As the girls get older that might get tricky unless we always go to the same place."

"That's a good thought. Let's keep that in mind and see what comes up. In the meantime, Howard said some contracts will be opening soon. Do you want to look at those with me Monday after school?"

I curled my legs up close. "Sure. No dice."

James laughed. "Right, no dice. How about we draw straws?"

"We could arm wrestle." I joked and gave him a little poke with my finger. I wasn't enthusiastic about playing games like we'd done before.

"Nope, you'd win. I never wrestle with a momma bear," James said and pulled the covers up higher. "She'd tear me to pieces."

I laughed and then sobered. "Can we stay home today? I need some time to think and maybe pray about everything." I'd wanted to throw the idea out and see what James might think about praying.

"Sounds good. I can even take the girls on a walk if you want some time to yourself," James offered.

He'd changed over the years, and now carried a softened approach where he put my needs ahead of his own instead of jumping at the next thing that crossed his mind. I'd also seen his tender ways with our girls, and it made me proud.

"Maybe." I closed my eyes and imagined sitting on the couch with a blanket and making some lists of criteria on school districts to choose from and a Christmas list for next month. Maybe I could have some input into our future as well as wherever we might land next.

CHAPTER 26

THE FOLLOWING SUMMER, JAMES OPTED FOR SEASONAL work in the city of Skagway, Alaska, working for the Customs Service. Together, we'd decided on this seasonal job in a remote part of the state. It was a dynamic location on the ocean but was also nestled in the mountains.

James rode the train in the summer from Skagway to Lake Bennett, checking passengers on their way to Skagway to board cruise ships.

We'd planned for our family to stay in Skagway for a teaching job, but then an opening came up for a one-room schoolhouse near Tok, which offered us the rural experience we enjoyed but was closer to what we were familiar with. Skagway was located in an area of Alaska where you had to travel through a portion of Canada to access it—or arrive via the ferry system—whereas Tok was on the Alaska Highway and just a few hours from Fairbanks.

It finally came time to leave Skagway. We packed up our few belongings and boarded the same train James had worked on all summer. Our train ride was a treat that day, since we rode as tourists.

As we headed to Whitehorse, Yukon, a stop on the way to

Chapter 26

Tok, I looked out the window at the mountains beside us. The fall colors splattered across the tree line and the mountaintops glistened with a dusting of snow. It was only early September, but winter was quickly approaching in this part of the north.

"Look girls, there's a moose eating his lunch in the pond!" James pointed out the window to a bull moose chomping on some grass with his head rising out of the water.

"It's still surreal to me that we have our car loaded on the train with us and that we're headed to Tok," I said as I gazed out the window at the spectacular view through the White Mountain Pass.

"Just another dream come true, sweets," James noted as he bounced Brooke on his lap before she slid down his leg to the floor.

"'Gain, Daddy," she said. She climbed back onto his lap, and he repeated the horsey ride, jiggling her on his knee until she slid off.

Another passenger walked past us, and her perfume reminded me of Marsha and the vanilla scent she wore. We'd kept in touch after their move.

"Do you think seeing Howard and Marsha while we're in Tok will really work sometime? Did you say it's about two-and-a-half hours by car to where they live in Glennallen?"

"We're practically neighbors," James said as he placed Brooke on the seat next to him.

"It would be so good to see them again," I said as I pulled out some crayons from my tote to give to Roberta, who had a coloring book on her lap. "It's too bad they left shortly after Thanksgiving for Glennallen. We were just getting to know them. But I understand why they were willing to go when the job opened sooner than they figured it would."

"I'll never forget their kindness," James replied.

"What do you think made them tick?" I asked.

James crossed his arms across his chest and slid back in the chair like he was positioning himself for a nap. "Um, what do you mean?"

"Marsha was always saying 'Thank God' and 'Dear Jesus,' like He was her friend next door. And when I was over making pies with her on our moving day, the entire family was saying Bible verses they'd memorized out loud. You and I both grew up going to church, but how she lived—like her heart was at peace with God—doesn't resonate with me."

"Mmm, yeah," James said sleepily. "Can we talk about it more… later? I'm…feeling the weight of the late nights." As he finished his sentence, he started to snore, and Brooke giggled at the sound.

I laughed too and placed my finger over my mouth, signaling to the girls to hush. The jostling of the train had a soothing effect on the girls too, and soon, they each curled up in their seats, mirroring their daddy. Thankfully, there'd be some quiet for me to get lost in my reflections of our next adventure: God and finding peace in it all.

AFTER GETTING OFF THE TRAIN, WE DROVE THE hundreds of miles to Tok with lots of singing and counting with the girls. Nearly three years old, their grandiose imaginations were easy to entertain, but only in short spurts.

Our contact in Tok had lined us up with a place to stay in Whitehorse for the night, and now we neared the outskirts of the small town.

"Remind me where the school is again?" I questioned James.

"It's about ten miles out of Tok on the way to Fairbanks. The guy said to pull over at the miler marker and he'll meet us there to give further directions."

"You'll be able to ask all the questions you had about the town two years ago when we stopped here," I said, remembering our return to the state and how the girls had both been crying, and I'd come close to losing it in the back of the van.

"All I can say is that there is a unique beauty for every area of Alaska we've lived. Especially here. It has a warm feeling. Do you sense that?" James asked as he pulled into the gas station on the corner.

"Give me some time, I guess. Last time we were here, the girls were screaming while you lingered in the Customs Office after we'd driven thousands of miles up the highway. I wasn't getting the warm fuzzies." My memory was sharp, and I'd not forgotten that day or the weight of the overwhelming tasks ahead of us.

After filling up, we pulled into the Customs Office and James ran in. Then, literally skipping his way back to the car, he jumped into the driver's seat. "How was that? Was I lightning fast this time?"

"Much better," I said and flashed him a wily grin.

Brooke and Roberta napped as we drove back onto the highway for the last stretch of road taking us to our next adventure.

The one-room schoolhouse at Tanacross sounded interesting, and James seemed up for the challenge. I wasn't sure how the girls and I would fit into the equation, but we had time to sort it out. Housing would be provided, and the weather was excellent for walks and exploring. The golden highway we would live near stood out most to me. It was a glistening treasure after a year of living in the bush.

"So, my lady, what is your one-word response to this Alaskan chance for the school year?" James pretended his fist was a microphone and held it out to me.

"Far out," I said with excitement and using modern-day terminology.

James put his arm on the back of my seat. "Oh, I like it."

We drove the rest of the way, commenting on the log homes along the highway and the Alaska Range in the southwest.

"Fred said to meet him at the pullout past the mile marker," James said. He turned the vehicle to the right and stopped close to a parked car on the road's edge.

"Fred? Is he with the school district?" I asked, uncertain of how all the pieces were coming together for our arrival at the rural school.

"He's a pastor," James said. "Look, that must be him."

A man was getting out of the car we'd parked behind. James got out and walked up to him. They shook hands, and the man, who I presumed was Fred, waved at me. James motioned for me to get out of the car. I peeked in the back at the soundly sleeping girls and stepped out.

"Hi! I'm Fred!" the man said as he walked toward me with a bounce to his step and his hand outstretched. "Nice to meet you."

"Nice to meet you too," I said as I looked around, assuming we'd be able to see the school by the road. "Is the school... here?" I asked.

Fred's laugh was friendly. "No, ma'am. I'm here to escort you there and show you the way. It's over the river and through the woods from here."

I laughed at his comment and smiled. It sounded like he would be an excellent tour guide. "All right, I guess we'll follow you there."

"Okay, let me know when you're ready," Fred said as he opened his car door and took his coat out. He pulled it on and put his hands in his pockets, looking between James and me.

James moved his eyes between Fred and his vehicle. "You can ride in our car if you'd like so you don't have to take yours, too."

"Uh-oh," Fred said. "You weren't told you can't drive there?"

"No," James stated and looked at me with his eyebrows raised.

Chapter 26

Should we have asked more questions? A school ten miles from Tok had sounded like near-heaven on earth.

"You won't need your car, just a good pair of boots." Fred pointed at his cowboy boots. "Need me to carry anything?" he asked and walked over to our car.

"If it's a short walk, we can come back for our things," James said. "Sharon, better go wake up the girls."

Fred spoke up. "Well, my friends, you're in for a treat. Few people around here get to have the pleasure of boating to their home nestled along the river."

Boat? River? I stood with my mouth open and searched James' face. Had he known these details? I turned and walked to the car to gather the girls and bundle them up. It was all more than I'd bargained for. My last boat ride had been when we'd fled our apartment during the flood.

I gulped back the lump in my throat. I could hear the men talking while I helped the girls out of the car and zipped their coats. Brooke shuffled along, looking at her feet while she walked, enthralled with the rubber boots we'd bought her before we moved to Skagway. They were still a fun treat for her after wearing mukluks all winter in Bethel. Roberta rubbed her eyes as she walked.

"Momma," Roberta said and reached up for me.

I picked her up and held Brooke's hand. I needed to draw on some strength to face the hop, skip, and a jump to our new home. Did the same God who drew Martha to Himself see the panic rising within me? Could He understand how I needed a mountain-sized portion of courage to persevere?

James must have sensed my reservations. He reached for Roberta and took her in his arms, then placed his other arm around my shoulder and gave me a kiss on the cheek.

"All right, this way," Fred exclaimed and walked over to a wide path at the edge of the pullout. "It's a short walk to the bank, then we'll take the boat over. Are you sure I can't carry anything for you?"

"We're okay," James answered for us.

We followed Fred's lead, and I whispered to James as we neared the river. "Did you know about this?" I nodded toward the water.

He mouthed the word *no*, then spoke up. "I pictured a bridge when they mentioned *across the river*."

At the water's edge, a rowboat was tied to a small dock. The water flowed to the west, and, downriver, I could see some buildings. Thank goodness it would not be a long ride, just a skirting across.

"Hop on in, and I'll row us over," Fred offered.

James helped me in, along with the girls, and I clutched them close.

Roberta repeated, "wa, wa."

"It's wa-ter, honey. Wa-ter," I repeated.

"I do the trip all the time. It's all part of the fun. Don't worry. The Mikels live in Tanacross as well, near where you'll be living. They're missionaries. I'm sure you'll meet them soon. Once they get back from their moose hunt." Fred rowed while he spoke and told us more about the river and how it flowed and dumped into the mighty Yukon up past Fairbanks.

I couldn't imagine how rowing from side to side was part of a casual trip to town. "Do you drive across in the winter?" I asked, curious if it was similar to the way people traveled near Bethel on the Kuskokwim from one village to the next.

"Yup," Fred said as we neared the edge.

"What's the name of the river again?" James questioned as Fred crouched in the boat before stepping out.

"The Tanana. The village is named Tanacross because you have to cross the Tanana River." He tied off the bow and reached to help us out. "If you want to look around for a bit, I'll go visit a few folks and meet you back here, James, and then we can get your things. Your place is there, next to the school. It's unlocked."

"Sounds good," James answered, and we walked hand in hand with the girls up to the large white building.

Each step flooded me with flashbacks of the years with James. Ohio to Fairbanks and back again with twin girls, a bush plane to Bethel, and a summer in Skagway. And now we'd committed to a new adventure that involved rowing across the river if we needed to get to the road.

My visits to Tok would be few if it meant traversing the water. There would have to be good reason to row across. And I might just drown in fear of the water's edge and how it would affect my ability to keep an eye on my girls?

CHAPTER 27

WE WORKED HARD TO BRIDGE THE CULTURAL GAP between us and the Native people we met in Tanacross. The school was the hub of the small community, and our house had the only telephone for the area.

The second month we were there, late in October, after the girls' third birthday, James organized a weekly movie night. Anyone who was around was welcome, but he mostly did it to connect with the kids.

One movie night, I set out popcorn on the counter and moved to the fridge to get the Kool-Aid I'd made earlier. I was all set for the fun to begin. Soon enough, James would be dancing along with the advertisements—something he loved to do. The girls joined in on the fun every time.

I shook my head at the memory of the week before when he'd had the whole room up and twisting and turning to the Bugs Bunny commercial. James' spunk was contagious, and it was hard to fathom that we'd arrived less than two months ago and had already made good connections with the kids, building their trust.

"Hey, sweets, looks good," James said as he rounded the

Chapter 27

corner from the hallway. "What about the other snacks I picked up while I was in Tok? Are we sharing them tonight?"

I tried not to stare him down. "James, those are for next week. We can't eat everything up so fast. Soon the river will be impassable, and then what? How long until the ice is thick enough to dare cross it?" I placed my hands on my hips. "And I don't plan on venturing out soon when it's barely frozen."

James dipped his hand into the popcorn bowl and tossed a few kernels in the air, trying to catch them in his mouth.

I closed my eyes and put my hand over them. "You're such a dweeb."

"I'm not socially inept."

I laughed.

"I know what dweeb means," he said. "I've had students look the word up when they use it in class." He walked over to me and put his hands on my shoulders. "C'mon, I'm groovy!"

"You're something all right," I answered. "Did you hear what I said about the ice?"

"Don't worry, we'll cross that bridge when we come to it. Oops, no pun intended." He moved back over to the counter and took another handful of popcorn.

James and his carefree ways. I was the opposite. My view of the river as a source of impending doom lingered over me like a black rain cloud. I'd told myself with each passing day that I'd get used to it. However, after a few trips on the boat, I still hadn't. My girls didn't seem to have any fear of the water or the dangerous force it represented.

With his mouth full of popcorn, James mumbled to me, "Mail."

"What?" I asked and turned to the sink to get a rag and wipe off the kitchen table—the crumbs from the girls' earlier sandwiches. I'd laid Brooke and Roberta down for a nap before the other kids arrived.

"The mail. It's still in a sack in the entryway. I was distracted when I got home and completely forgot. We've a box and some letters."

Every few days, at least, someone in town traveled to Tok, picked up the mail for the community, and handed it out.

I hurried to the entryway, pulled the bag into the center of the living room and dug in. Only a few packages had arrived for us over the years. What had been sent to us here?

"Wow, you're like a little kid at Christmas," James said. He came over to hold the sack open while I removed the box out from the bottom.

"I know," I said with enthusiasm. "Huh, it says fragile on it. I hope they carried it with care." I pulled the tape back, revealing the return address. "Hmm, it postmarked from Ohio. Do you think Mary sent us something?"

"Nope. There's a letter from her here in the bag." James pulled out a few envelopes and sorted them in his hand.

Pulling back the tape farther, I saw my parents' address. "It's from my folks," I said as I drew open the top and removed a card. I sat down, legs crisscrossed on the shag rug in the middle of the room, and read out loud.

Dear James, Sharon, and girls.

We decided since you were settling into a new location, we'd send a few of your things bit by bit to help make your house a home. I hope you don't mind, Sharon, but I picked a box out of storage and sent it to you without confirming the contents. You'd labeled the box "dishes." We miss you lots and look forward to seeing pictures of the girls sometime.

Love, Mom and Dad.

I set the card down. "Aw, such a sweet idea," I said and sighed.

"I'd forgotten about the boxes we left at your parents' place. Guess we should send money to have them send a few now and then," James suggested as he took a seat on the couch and opened the envelopes. "This one is from Mary." He held up an envelope. "And she sent some coloring pages for the girls."

Chapter 27

"So sweet of her," I stated, before pulling up a layer of tissue and removing the first item from the box. "It's...it's a frame." I turned it over. "It's the cross-stitched one we opened with Mary," I said with enthusiasm, remembering the day we opened the gift. I read the verse on the front aloud. "Trust in the Lord with all thine heart; and lean not unto thine own understanding. In all thy ways acknowledge Him, and He shall direct thy paths." I looked up at James and smiled. "I'd forgotten all about it. We have certainly zigzagged our paths since then."

"Huh, that's for sure," James said.

I set the frame on the coffee table and removed the next layer of tissue, revealing freesia petal teacups I'd packed years ago.

"Oh my!" I said, "look how beautiful and delicate these are! My Mom couldn't have picked a more fragile box than this one." I traced the flower on the cup with my fingertip.

The world of tea in the afternoon and casual walks along city sidewalks seemed so foreign now that we'd grown accustomed to wooded paths and backyard bonfires. Our lives were so different.

"What is it, sweets?" James asked.

"James?" I questioned. "I've tried it all." I gulped back the lump in my throat and tears welled up in my eyes. "We've traversed the country twice, we've lived all over the state, survived a flood, and through it all I've prayed to God, called out to Him, and my cup is still empty."

Coming full-circle to holding untouched wedding gifts drove home the point that I still wasn't who I wanted to be. Had anything in my life changed through the storms we'd endured?

James came and kneeled next to me and wiped the tears from my eyes. "I'm not sure I understand."

"Where? James, where?" I put my head on his shoulder and let the sobs release. "Where can I find peace? I've tried to be a good wife and mom and to please my parents, and I still can't find it. I just want to know it's all going to be okay."

"Shh, Sharon. Shh." James stroked my hair and pulled me in tighter. "You are going to be okay. You are."

I let his words speak to me, and I tried to grab onto them with my mind and let them settle in. But there was another missing puzzle piece that I couldn't explain to James. It needed to be addressed because, in all of our adventures, I hadn't managed to find it. How did the Sonnet of Sad end? What was the answer?

A knock on the door sent me springing to my feet, and I took the box to the kitchen.

I'd need to fill the gap in my understanding with something. If nothing else, for the sake of my girls who had wandered from their room and now stood at the edge of the hall staring at me.

THE PINK SHADOWS OF A SUNSET CAST THEIR COLOR onto the snow. I looked out the window and back to the clock on the wall. It was almost three in the afternoon. Daylight was short in December, but spectacular. I'd told Mary in a letter that it was like a long sunrise followed by a slow sunset full of color and brilliance.

We'd settled into a routine across the river, and it had been weeks since I'd been to Tok. My world had become very mundane, and very small. Yesterday, when I'd overheard kids talking about a missionary family coming to visit, they'd spoken with so much excitement that I could hardly wait to meet them myself. From what James and I could make out from his older students, the family would be hosting an after-school club for a week.

Finally, the day had come.

"Brooke and Roberta, come here. It's time to bundle up and go to the school," I called loudly down the hall so the girls could hear me. Even though it was a short walk, we needed to bundle up in all our winter gear: long parkas with fur ruffs and moccasins we'd purchased in Bethel from locals. The girls each had a pair of rabbit-fur mittens that they loved. They'd often play with them inside the house and pretended they were their pets.

"Yes, Momma," I heard Brooke say as she ran into the living room and threw herself onto the couch cushion. "I go see Daddy?" she asked and came over to me.

"Mm, hm, yes, honey," I said as I wrestled her coat on. "And today we'll go and visit with the kids too."

"Yay!" she said and jumped up and down.

"Roberta," I called out. "Momma said for you to come."

I pushed Brooke's mittens onto her little hands. Covered from head to toe with the bulky winter gear, she looked like a marshmallow. Style wasn't even a consideration when the temps dropped to near forty below. Warmth was of utmost importance.

I could hear Roberta's tiny, leisurely steps coming down the hall.

"Roberta, you need to listen to Momma. Daddy is waiting." The ever-increasing demands of the duo three-year-olds was a surprise to me. I'd assumed the terrible twos was the dreaded time where toddlers learned the word no. However, since turning three, the girls had asserted their wills even more.

She rounded the corner and moved at a snail's pace to where I stood holding out her coat. I didn't hold back a stern look. "C'mon, your sister is going to sweat it out with her coat on, waiting for you."

I helped Roberta with her gear, then put on my own. I was still buttoning my coat when Brooke pushed the door to the entryway open. *How did she do that?* It should have been latched shut so she wouldn't be able to enter with a simple push. How had I overlooked closing it properly?

"You can wait in there if you like, honey. Momma will be right there."

Roberta followed Brooke's lead and headed out the door as well while I pushed my feet into my boots and grabbed my insulated coffee thermos. Having a hot drink once we arrived would help keep my blood flowing.

Together, we walked down the entryway steps and out into the wintry afternoon. The humidity from our breath froze in the air, and the girls giggled while they hopped and skipped along.

Our path to the school took us near the river's edge. I'd established a routine with them where we respected the river and kept our distance. Still, they always found a reason to want to move closer.

"Look!" Roberta shouted. "Wabbit!"

A large white rabbit jumped in front of us, then hopped over near the river. Roberta chased it, and I called out to her.

"No! Stay there." I picked up my pace so I would be near her. "Daddy's waiting," I reminded her.

They both loved time with their daddy, and I hoped to help keep them on track with that mission. I was also eager to meet the family that the kids had spoken so highly of.

Eventually, Roberta veered back, closer to Brooke, and we made our way to the school.

Once inside with the girls, I scanned the entryway and the large common area for the missionaries. Where were they from?

Before I could redirect the girls to look for James, they ran down the hall to the where he usually was after school: the gym. As the basketball coach, he already had kids practicing after school to prepare for the opening of the season later in the month.

I picked up the girls' things and hung them on hooks near the entry, then put my gear close to theirs. As I turned around, I saw a young woman kneeling down and talking to a young girl. She listened intently to her, nodding, and then they hugged.

When she stood up, she walked over to me, outstretching

Chapter 27

her hand. "Hi, I'm Lois. My husband, Tom, is around here somewhere."

"Hi," I replied. "I'm Sharon, James' wife."

"Nice to meet you. We've met James already and have club set up in the gym. I hope you came to stay. You can help me with a couple of things if you like."

"Sure. Our girls are three. Is it okay if they join in?"

"Absolutely. I'm so glad you brought them. I've heard they're dolls."

I cleared my throat. "When we moved to Tanacross, we heard that missionaries lived here and were out hunting, but we've never seen them. Um, if it's you they were talking about…"

Lois laughed. "You'll find most everyone knows everyone's business here." She shrugged her shoulders. "And I don't mind. Yes, that was probably us. After we went hunting downriver, we traveled outside to a missions conference. We're back now, just in time for winter."

"Outside?' I questioned, unsure of what she meant.

She put her hand on her forehead. "Ah, I do that all the time. It's a term used in Alaska meaning outside of Alaska. Not sure where it came from. Sorry for the confusion. I've noticed it's used more commonly in the rural parts of the state."

We walked together to the gym, where the kids ran around playing tag. Brooke and Roberta stood watching the older children while James tried using a ball to coax them closer to play with the students.

Lois gave a high whistle, and all the kids froze. "Great job!" she shouted out. "You remembered. C'mon on over and sit in a circle and let's go over the rules."

The children sat obediently, listened to her review, and held up their hands in queue to answer her questions. They welcomed her commanding presence. She'd gained their respect.

I took a seat over to the side while Lois started a game. Then her husband came into the gym and took over. She wandered over to me. "Want to help me with the snack? It's next. We keep them busy eating while we tell our Bible story. This way we have their undivided attention. It's harder to talk with food in your mouth."

"Okay. It's nice of you to bring a snack. Food is harder to bring over here from Tok now." I'd a new appreciation for anything extra.

"It's our pleasure. It's the least we can do. It could be part of what wins over a soul, you know?" She nudged me as we walked to the corner of the room where she had some supplies.

I didn't know what she meant. Winning over a soul?

"It's so nice to have a young family here," she continued. "Will you and James stay for a bit?" She pulled out some boxed milk from a crate as she spoke.

"Um, I haven't gotten used to it here enough to say whether we'll stay," I said quietly.

Although we felt settled and the adventure of it all was captivating, I'd lain awake at night, mulling over my sense of purpose in it all. I fought in earnest to find a foundation to build upon. I'd checked the boxes for serving my family, but what else was there? There was still that missing puzzle piece.

"Sounds like the students love you and James. Earlier today, they were telling me about the movie nights you have and how James is going to coach basketball. How exciting. These kids don't get opportunities like these from every teacher. You're a gift to them." She handed me some paper bags. "Speaking of gifts, these are a little something for everyone to take home, if you don't mind setting them aside."

I moved the paper bags to a table and then followed Lois back over to the group.

The kids sat in a circle, and Lois' husband held up an oversized cardboard book. "Who can tell me what the gold page stands for?" he asked, and an older boy raised his hand.

The story continued while Tom quizzed the kids about the

book, which had no words, only colors. Each page represented something different.

"And the dark page reminds us of the fact that we've all sinned. Can anyone give me an example of sin?"

A little girl who I'd watched play with my girls held her hand high and Lois' husband called on her.

"It's like when I don't come when my mom says to. Or when my brother lies."

Lois chimed in and stood next to her husband. "Let's do the motions, everyone, and say it together. Sin is anything we think, say, or do that separates us from God. Good job on remembering the hand signals for that one."

Mesmerized by the unique club and distracted by helping Lois, I'd neglected to look around for Brooke and Roberta. I'd assumed James was watching them, but he stood over in the corner, talking to one of his high school students. I scanned the circle of kids and didn't see them sitting among the group.

My steps quickened as I jogged out of the gym into the hall. Where were they?

"Brooke! Roberta!" I called out, assuming they'd be nearby.

I ran down to the large classroom, my heart pounding. Would they have gone looking for their daddy in his room? When I didn't find them there, I turned and ran to the entryway. The door to the school was open and the cold air was rushing in.

CHAPTER 28

I PUSHED THE FRONT DOOR WIDE OPEN AND STEPPED out into the cold in my stockinged feet. "Brooke! Roberta!" I called out, scanning the schoolyard. There wasn't any sign of them. Why had I assumed they'd left? Second-guessing my reaction, I ran down the hall to the gym, yelling for James.

As I rounded the corner, I bumped into him.

"What's the matter?" he asked, his eyes wide.

"I can't find the girls." I fired out the words in a panic, trying to catch my breath.

"They're right there," he said as he pointed to the bleachers.

I slumped my shoulders and hung my head. Why had I reacted in such a panic? "How did I miss them? I looked here, and in your classroom, and then I saw the front door was open. I...I assumed they'd wandered outside and—"

James placed his arms around my shoulder, and we walked to the girls, who stood playing with some squishy balls, oblivious to the terror that had ripped me to my core. I sat next to them, and James returned to the sidelines with a group of teens.

The school kids erupted in cheers in the center of the gym and stood up, giving each other high fives. Lois walked over to me. "Your girls are such cuties. Did you say they're three?"

I gulped, trying to hold back the explosion of fear pulsating through my body. "Yes, their birthday is in October." Diverting my gaze to the girls, I smiled at the chatter between them.

"Are you okay?" Lois asked, stepping closer.

"I, uh, I couldn't find the girls and ran around in a panic. Somehow I didn't see them here." I pulled back the wisp of hair that had fallen near my face. "I feel so foolish."

"Oh, momma bear," she stated. "I've done that many times myself, and then I thanked God everyone was fine. It's all part of being a mom. The innate and powerful protective force driving you is God-given. He's entrusted these girls to you." She sat next to them and clapped with Roberta, who'd initiated patty cake with her.

He'd entrusted them to me? He trusted me to watch over them? There's no way I could watch them every minute. Obviously, I'd lost my oversight today. "I don't know that I trust myself, never mind being able to carefully directing them at all times."

Finishing her song with Roberta, Lois looked over at me. "I don't mean it that way." She smiled widely. "It's more like He has given them to you for a season. They won't always be little. Now is the time to train them and help set a course for the rest of their lives. You've already begun the process—the moment you conceived them. And remember, God is a constant, powerful presence. He watches over our kids all the time."

I picked up some blocks that the girls had dumped out of the toy-tote I carried on our outings for them. "How many kids do you have?" I asked Lois.

"We've four kiddos. Our oldest is at college in Glennallen at Alaska Bible School. The second oldest is in high school, and the two youngest are in junior high." She pointed across the room. "They're over next to Tom helping to hand out miniature wordless books to the kids. My daughter is sixteen and the twins are fourteen."

My ears perked at the mention of twins. "Oh, you must've been busy when they were young—with two older kids."

Lois bent over to pick up the miscellaneous items on the floor. "Yes, I was. Not sure I could have kept my head on straight if it wasn't for God's strength. I'd better go help Tom finish the club. Thanks for your hand earlier—with the snacks. We live in a log cabin on the edge of town. Do you want to visit some more tomorrow?"

"I'd like that. And thanks for coming and doing the club with the kids." I waved my hands toward the group standing around the missionary family. "They were so excited for you to come."

"Our pleasure. Not sure how I overlooked it, but tomorrow is church in Tok. We'll be back later in the afternoon. Hey, would you and your family like to come with us?"

"I'll check with James." I gulped remembering the last time we'd been to church and how I'd felt inadequate for not teaching my girls about God.

"No pressure. If you want to come, be at the dock by nine."

I shuddered. "Hmm, it's chilly in here." I tried to cover my reaction. "Okay."

"All right. Hopefully, we'll see you tomorrow, either at the dock or later in the afternoon."

"Bye," I said and helped the girls walk to the entryway. James would stay for basketball practice, and I needed to go home, make a cup of coffee and decide how to muster up the courage to go to church.

WE MET THE MIKEL FAMILY AT THE DOCK AND PILED into their van for the drive across the river and into town. James had assured me the ice had frozen to a safe depth and families had crossed a couple of weeks ago. On our way home, James would start up our car and bring it back to the house. That morning, the thermometer read thirty below. It hardly seemed possible that the wheels could turn at this temperature, never mind carry us over the ice and onto the highway.

I positioned myself in the middle seat with the girls and checked their winter gear was still on properly. Their moccasins were strapped on tight, and I'd pushed their fur mittens on snugly. Pulling my scarf higher over my nose, I smiled at Lois when she climbed inside and sat ahead of me.

"Hey there! You're no chechako, are you? All bundled up in your furs and ready to take on the Alaska ice road. What a brave soul," Lois said, tugging at Brooke's toes.

Brooke waved at her and clapped. "Hi," she said in her small voice.

"I've not heard that one before. What's a chechako?" The van lurched forward, and I placed my hands on the seat in front of me as though I was holding myself in the vehicle.

James turned in his front seat next to Tom and gave me a thumbs up.

"Oh, sorry," said Lois. "It means a newcomer to Alaska. You surpassed it long ago. I heard you lived in the bush? And you were in Fairbanks when the flood hit. I'd love to hear your stories."

I didn't see the superhero element of our lives. We'd ended up where we had by shrugging our shoulders at chance. Still, I figured I should agree because I wanted to hear her stories a well.

"Sure," I replied.

The van bumped along the ice, which was rough, and the jostling sent my pulse racing. I closed my eyes and took a deep breath, then looked down at the girls. They played carefree, without a fleeting worry. I concentrated on watching them and pretended I needed to tighten Brooke's moccasin. As I finished the last bow in her leather laces, we were on land again.

We visited on the way to Tok, and turned left toward a little white church with a tall steeple rising to the blue, clear sky. Hm, the memory of the church we'd been married in came to mind. It had a similar steeple.

Our wedding seemed like a lifetime ago. Rolling the dice at our rehearsal had set the trajectory for our Alaskan life. Now, with two girls in tow, we forged our way. Little did I know at the time where the number six would take me: the tundra, the Delta of the Kuskokwim River, and a teaching outpost off the beaten path.

James and Tom came around to the side of the van and helped the girls and me out. We followed as the Mikels filed into the church ahead of us through the double doors at the front. Faith Chapel, it said on the sign out front. *Faith* sounded like something that might be promising. Perhaps this church held answers. As we walked in and removed our long coats, a familiar face greeted us.

"Hi, James. Hi, Sharon," Fred said with enthusiasm. "Nice to see you." He reached to shake James' hand. "C'mon in and find a seat. It's nice and warm in here."

We sat down with the Mikels near the front. The girls looked up at the bright lights overhead, and as I pulled Roberta onto my lap, I whispered, "Remember, honey, we need to be quiet in church."

Fred walked to the front. "Good morning, everyone," he said cheerfully. "Will you please rise for our first song? You'll find it in your hymnals."

I fumbled with the book, searching for the right number while balancing Roberta on my lap. She reached for the hymnal as well. How did people juggle kids and church? We stood up, and I tried to sing along with the song that was obviously familiar to the congregation. They were singing it beautifully. It had been such a long time since I'd heard a chorus of voices singing.

I chimed in at the beginning once I'd found where we were:

. . .

Standing, standing,
> Standing on the promises of God, my Savior;
> Standing, standing,
> I'm standing on the promises of God.

Roberta tugged at my skirt. "Momma."
> I sshed her and carried on.

Standing on the promises that cannot fail.
> When the howling storms of doubt and fear assail,
> By the living Word of God I shall prevail,
> Standing on the promises of God.

The words "living Word of God" caught my attention, and I wondered at the concept of it being alive? What did it mean?

Fred led the singing with the exuberant hand motions of a conductor, and we carried on with verse three. I glanced over at James, who sang along.

Standing on the promises of Christ, the Lord,
> Bound to Him eternally by love's strong cord,
> Overcoming daily with the Spirit's sword,
> Standing on the promises of God.

As we sang the chorus, I was puzzled by what "the Spirit's sword" meant. I peered at the faces of church members, who sang the music in unison. The last verse began.

. . .

Standing on the promises I cannot fall,
   List'ning ev'ry moment to the Spirit's call,
   Resting in my Savior as my all in all,
   Standing on the promises of God.

We sat down and sang another unfamiliar song before Fred opened his Bible and spoke. He seemed comfortable behind the wooden pulpit at the front of the church—his shoulders squared back and his head held high.

"I have a question for you today as we lead into the sermon. Raise your hand if you've ever played the board game Life." He looked around the congregation. "Ah, I see many of you have. Aren't you glad we don't have to live our lives by the roll of the dice, whether we land on a new car or add a pink or a blue baby peg to the back of our old car?"

I gulped and looked over at James, who gave me a wink.

Fred continued with his talk about life. "Folks"—he moved from behind the pulpit and stood in front of it—"you don't know how to live until you learn how to die." He turned and walked back. "Life isn't a game." He opened his Bible on the pulpit. "Let me explain. Please turn with me in your Bibles to the book of Ecclesiastes."

He read some verses I'd never heard before. I'd not learned of Ecclesiastes. The church I'd gone to as a girl was more rote and ritualistic. I'd read aloud the prayers in unison. The exposition of verses here was an experience I'd never had before. I strained to not only listen, but to understand what Fred was trying to get across to us.

"The verse tells us more about our situation as humans before a Holy God. We have deep-seated flaws. Therefore, without Him, we cannot think clearly about our relationship with Him. Not until we understand the greatness of our sin.

"You know, the things we do and say which oppose God?

They affect how we think and feel. But the good news is this, my friends"—

he leaned forward and scanned the people in the chapel, and a smile grew across his face—"the Bible shines in the darkness and makes sense of it all!" He gently tapped the pulpit with his palm. "It's the light to your mind to show you the truth. You were made to understand your grand purpose in life."

He moved in front of the pulpit and walked back and forth with his arms behind his back, studying the crowd. "Have you ever felt homesick, and you're at home? I have. It's the strangest thing. You look around"—he looked over his shoulders, then back at us all—"and you may ask yourself, 'what am I missing?'"

How did he know how I felt? It was as though he was speaking directly to my soul. I gulped.

"We will never feel at home here because it's not where we are destined to spend eternity. God wants to have a personal relationship with you forever. Not just some afternoon over coffee or while you go for a walk in the woods and say, 'wow, those mountains are really neat.' He offers you an intimate, personal relationship with Him."

Fred pointed to the back of the room, then from one pew to another. He didn't speak in a mocking tone, but with sincerity, and a smile spread across his face. "When we leave our life to chance like in the game of Life, it leaves us frustrated because our destiny is uncertain. Would you like to know, today, how you can be assured of a relationship with God forever?"

I heard my heart say yes, and I leaned forward, wanting to grasp what Fred was saying.

"I'd like to invite you to receive this free gift that God wants to give you. Jesus is the one who bridges the gap between your sin and God. He paid the penalty for your sin so that you can have a relationship with Him forever. Will you bow your heads with me now? and I'll pray."

Fred prayed and talked to God like He was in the room with

us. I felt a sensation within me, as though I'd discovered a valuable treasure—like Fred had exposed a vein of gold in the hills. I wanted to know more. Questions rolled through my mind, and I clasped my hands tight. I needed to understand. Could I change the way I was thinking and acting?

Fred ended his prayer with a statement. "And, God, please help anyone here who has never heard the Good News decide, today, to be part of your family. Before it's too late."

Too late? I opened my eyes and looked over at James, who sat with his eyes closed. Where had the time crunch come from? What was the urgency? I pulled Brooke, who'd fallen asleep on my lap, closer. For the sake of my family, was there something we needed to do? Perhaps I'd missed something.

I breathed my prayer. *God, I want to find you. I'm looking. Amen.*

The service ended, and people got up to visit. James held Roberta, who slept in his arms, and I stayed seated with Brooke sprawled across the pew. A familiar voice next to me caught my attention.

Someone tapped me on the shoulder. "Sharon?"

I turned to see Martha from Bethel. "Hi!" I exploded with excitement as the site of her.

"I thought I recognized you from where I was sitting. My, your girls have grown so much!" She came and sat next to me and gave me a side hug.

"Do you still live in Glennallen?" I asked.

"We do. Our church is deeply intertwined with Faith Chapel and all the missionary work Fred has going on. It's like one enormous family. We come up here often and go with him on some of his trips, flying up to Chicken on Saturday to host a kids club similar to Sunday school. Do you and James live here now?" She looked around and smiled at James, who stood talking to another couple I didn't recognize.

"No, we live across the river. James is teaching there this year. It's so good to see you."

"You're quite the trooper, Sharon. You've gone from Bethel to here. I'm impressed with your fortitude to live remotely and make the best of it. I'm sure it's difficult."

How had she seen into my soul? My life wasn't easy.

Parts of it were.

But other parts weren't.

The worst was my search for peace in it all. It tore at me like a wolf on a caribou. Exposing my wounds of fear and worry.

"We came with the Mikels. Do you know them?" I questioned.

"Yes, I do. We've known each other for years. They've been missionaries in Alaska for some time now. Tom speaks at the Bible College in Glennallen sometimes."

"Alaska is such a small world, among you church people." As I spoke, I wished I could take back my words and eat them. I'd sounded brisk.

Marsha smiled. "Well, we are like family. You know, I have a book I've been rereading. It has helped me through some difficult situations. Perhaps it's something you'd find helpful. Actually, I have a copy with me. Fred was handing out copies the last time I was here, and I brought back the extras."

"Sure," I answered before I gave it any thought.

Marsha got up and walked to the back of the church. Brooke squirmed, then stretched in place on the pew. My girls were not growing up hearing about God or the Bible. What direction were we steering them? If I didn't know where I was headed, how could I possibly align their lives with assurance?

CHAPTER 29

WHEN JAMES WOKE UP ON NEW YEAR'S DAY, HE greeted the morning with, "How'd we get so lucky to live in a place like this?"

After breakfast, he took the girls sledding while I sat by the woodstove to read the book Marsha had shared with me. I looked up from the front cover and watched the snow gently falling outside the large picture window in our living room.

I was thankful he'd taken the girls so I could have some time to myself. I curled my legs under me and repositioned the blanket. These short winter days with little daylight were cozy. My coffee mug was full and sitting on the end table next to me. Flipping open the book, I read the title page, the dedication, then the first chapter.

It explained that there is a ladder of expectation where we anticipate having the correct emotions about a situation and will want to act on those innate senses.

Isn't that how we're wired? I asked myself. "Especially as a mom," I stated out loud. I often didn't consider my response to a situation. Instead, I went right into action.

I kept reading, tracking with my eyes the diagram showing a linear pattern of facts first, then faith and how emotions follow.

It made sense. I reached for my coffee, then let the statement take root as I sipped my hot drink.

So, what were the facts that I needed to get straight? The question pressed me on as I read and reread the brief chapter.

There was a call to prayer at the end—to confess my sin to God and see my need for Him. Had I understood it correctly? There it was, written in words, with a diagram and Bible verses to highlight the progression. It sounded similar to what Fred had shared on Sunday.

No, it *was* what he shared! How had I not heard it fully?

I stood up and walked over to the window, watching even larger flakes fall to the ground. We'd heard on the radio that a winter storm would begin that night. *It must be blowing in early.*

Last year in Bethel, I'd done a study with the kids about snowflakes and how each one is unique and special. We'd made our own snowflakes out of paper and taped them to the windows as a reminder of how we were each unique. The snow falls with purity and perfection, and it isn't dirtied or squished until it lands on the ground. It was a beautiful representation of each person's individuality.

Taking a step back, I blinked. How had I shaded my eyes from the very lesson I was teaching others? I was the same. I was unique. And I wanted a purpose. I wanted to know I was special.

I'd kicked my slippers off under the table at breakfast. Now, my feet felt a little cool, so I slipped them back on before moving back to the couch.

I sat down and looked around the room. Blessings surrounded me. James was an amazing husband and father, serving and loving us. My girls were amiable and excelling in their speech and physical development. Our parents were supportive of our life in Alaska, and Mary made regular trips to visit us and spoil the girls. I had a great life. Why did God matter?

My questions were interrupted by stomping on the stairs, and the door flew open. James gasped for breath. "Sharon"—he breathed in and out—"the girls"—he held his chest with his hand—"they're gone."

I jumped up and ran to him. "What?"

As I listened, I grabbed my coat and stuffed my feet in my boots. "We were at the hill, and I was building a little fire to roast some hotdogs." He drew in deep breaths. "I saw them piling snow in the sled over by the hill. Then"—

He gulped.

I saw the tears in his eyes, and he placed a hand on my shoulder.

—"Let's hurry."

I stuffed my hands in my mittens, grabbed my hat, and shut the door behind me. How could they be missing? Bile rose in the back of my throat and there was pressure rising in my chest. Would I be able to breath?

The gently falling snow had turned into a fierce blizzard. In Ohio, these types of storms blew in with impending doom. My heart raced at the memory. What could we even see?

I FOLLOWED JAMES' FOOTSTEPS TO THE HILL BEHIND the school, pierced by the thought that we might be moving farther and farther away from them each second, even though it was a short distance from the house. As he hurried, he called out for the girls. Turning around to look, I saw our footprints were quickly filling in from the falling snow and now the blowing wind. It reminded me of an Ohio winter, where a prairie storm could reduce visibility within minutes.

Oh God, help, God. Help us see.

We came close to the hill and near to the Mikels' cabin. I called out to James. "I'm going to ask for help!"

Chapter 29

He nodded to me. "I'll meet you at the hill." James took off running.

I yelled as I stepped up to their door. "Help! It's the girls. Help!" I knocked on their door, then opened it. Lois, who was at the door, took a step back and stared at me. "The girls?" she asked.

"Yes, James was at the sledding hill with them. They're gone. Can you help?"

Lois grabbed my hands. "Dear Jesus, help us find the girls. Point us in the right direction. Shine Your light so we can see them. Amen." She turned and yelled. "Tom, get the kids! Go ahead, Sharon, we'll be right there."

I scrambled out the door and ran as best I could through the deep snow behind their house to the hill. Why would my girls have wandered off? Could someone have taken them?

Please let them be safe. Please help us find them. God, You know. You know. Tears flowed, and I pushed forward to the hill. James stood at the base, and I could hear him talking to several others.

Running to me, James called out, "I sent them in all four directions, and I'm going to stay here because maybe they'll come back. I don't know what else to do! You can't see their footprints anymore," James cried. "Sharon!"

I reached for James and gave him a hug. "I'm going to the river, James.'

"What?" He held my forearms and searched my face.

"I can't get it out of my mind. I have to look there."

"Take Lois with you," he said as she approached with Tom and the kids.

"Where?' Lois asked.

"To the river!" I grabbed her arm and pulled her toward me. We followed the trail through the woods to the river—the ice road: the most dangerous place I could imagine for my three-year-old daughters.

We ran, and Lois prayed out loud. "Help us God, You're with us, Jesus. Show us the way to them."

She talked to God like He was ahead of us, looking over His shoulder, motioning us to follow. A loving Heavenly Father showing the way.

We approached the river. I couldn't see the other side. There was a gnawing deep inside me, pushing me to search across the ice. Why was I drawn to look, when I couldn't see a viable reason to?

"What were they wearing?" Lois asked.

"They had their parkas on and—oh—their bright kuspuks over top of them. One is wearing purple and the other pink." I clasped my hands and then rubbed them. My knees felt weak. Was it all the running?

God, which way?

"I'll go this way to the right and call for them. You go that way and call. Look at the ice and overflow and watch for any sign that they may have tried to bridge the river."

I nodded and fought back a gasping sob rising to the surface. My babies. I needed to find them.

Lead me, God.

Lois squeezed my hand, then we went separate directions. I studied the ground as I walked, scanning and examining the snow's surface for any clue. Then I called their names calmly. Maybe we were scaring them with our yelling. "Brooke, Roberta. Mommy wants to go sledding with you. Brooke, Roberta. Mommy can make hot chocolate for you. Brooke, Roberta…"

I repeated myself a couple more times, then noticed a crushed drift without mounds of freshly fallen snow atop it. My gaze darted out from there across the ice. There were some small imprints filling with snow. The tracks must be fresh. I followed them and quickened my pace. "Roberta. Brooke." I tried to sound enticing to them. "Honey, it's time to go home. Time for a snack."

Chapter 29

Help me be calm, God, and see what I need to. Help them hear me even though the wind is howling.

I followed the trail to the black spruce at the edge of the other side. It was our meeting spot, where we gathered on the road's side of the river before we crossed. I looked up and down the river's edge, then walked into the woods. "Brooke! Roberta!"

I heard a faint noise, like a calf moose making a low cry for its momma.

"Honey?" I turned ninety degrees. "Are you there?" My gaze darted from tree to tree, searching and hoping.

"Momma," the small voice said.

My eyes landed on the two girls huddled under a large pine tree. I ran to them, tears pouring down my face. "Brooke, Roberta! Momma's here!" Falling to my knees, I enveloped them in a hug. "Momma's here!" My body softened in relief, yet I gripped them tight. "Momma is here."

"Thank YOU, Jesus!" I said. "Thank you, thank you." And I rocked my girls, clinging to them.

"Momma,' Brooke's muffled voice said.

"Yes, honey?"

"We'z trying to go to church. Is this the way, Momma?"

"Honey, we will always go to church together." I brushed back the wet hair falling across her eyes. "C'mon, now let's go find your daddy and tell him that Jesus showed me where you were."

"He did?" Roberta questioned.

"Yes, baby girl, He did!"

We walked together, and once we were on the river, I called out, "They're safe! We're safe."

God had shown me where to find my girls. *He's what I need because He will take care of my girls when I can't. And He will take care of me.*

❄

THE MIKELS OPENED THEIR HOME TO US AND THE search party. Lois made hot chocolate, and her kids pulled out games. We sat in their living room with the girls asleep on the floor at our feet, exhausted from their adventure to "go find church."

"I'm so glad they're okay." I shook my head in disbelief at how the day had turned from picturesque to horrifying.

James sat next to me on the couch, pulled me in close, and whispered, "I'm so sorry."

I lifted my head. "It's over now. And we're all okay."

"Gosh, that's a parent's worst fear," James said as he ran his hand through his hair. "They vanished in a nanosecond. I don't suppose it will be okay to make them ride strapped into the sled for rest of the winter, will it?" he teased.

Tom walked over from the kitchen, carrying two mugs, then handed one to James and one to me. "Probably not, but I don't blame you. Our youngest twin went missing once when we were out-of-state, and I wanted to give him a piggyback ride the rest of his life."

With my drink in my hand, I stood and walked over to the kitchen and sat on one of their stools at the u-shaped counter. "I started the book Marsha gave me," I announced to Lois as she ran the kitchen rag under the running water.

"Oh? What do you think?" she asked and wrung out the rag, then wiped the counter next to the stove.

"It makes sense." I folded my hands around my mug, savoring the warmth.

"Would you like to meet sometime and chat about it?" she offered as she folded the rag on edge of the sink.

"I'd like that," I answered.

There was much I admired about my new friend. My feelings toward her were not a harsh envy, but a heartfelt yearning to have what she had. I wasn't far from being where I'd been trying to get.

I was ready.

There was a new beginning ahead of me, like the fresh idea of a New Year's wish. Except mine wasn't a wish, it was growing layer upon layer from a firm foundation. I was going to stand on the promises of God.

CHAPTER 30

Lois volunteered to take me to Tok and out for an afternoon during James' vacation from school. We drove into town, stopping first at the post office, and then we came to the steepled Faith Chapel. I gazed once again at the cross perched on top and smiled. The way had been pointed out to me long ago. I hadn't had the eyes to see it.

Inside the entry, we stomped the snow off our feet, walked into the sanctuary and sat at the back. As we'd strolled in, Lois mentioned that the church doors were always open.

"I come in here sometimes and enjoy the quiet," Lois said. "Other times, I play the piano and sing." She closed her eyes. "But it doesn't matter, you can worship God anywhere." Lois pulled her boots off and tucked her feet underneath her. "Tell me about the book and where you are at."

"I'm done," I said as I set it between us and smoothed the cover.

"Fast reader," Lois said.

"I was thirsty." I picked up the Bible from the wooden holder on the pew in front of me.

"The ladder was the picture I needed in my mind. The bridge, the cross, it all makes sense now."

Chapter 30

Lois picked up the backpack she'd set on the floor and pulled out her Bible. The pages looked worn, and the cover was barely holding on by a thread. "Can you remind me?"

"It's the facts. First, the facts of who God is and what His character means. He's a holy God, and He wants to have a relationship with us. "But"—I put up one finger—"we are sinful, and we can't be in His presence with our sin. So"—I held up another finger—"He made a way to bridge the gap. Those are the facts.

"We want to feel like we can earn his love and work to please Him, but it's counterproductive. It only breeds fear and worry of acceptance. I know, because that's how I've been living—trying to include Him but not knowing how."

Lois pulled out a booklet from her bag and placed it on her Bible. "We share the wordless book with the kids at the club and use colors to show these truths. You've shared the dark page of sin, and at that point in the book, we share the red page signifying blood. There had to be a sacrifice to atone for our sin. This is where Jesus fills the gap—the distance between us and God—and brings us peace with God, knowing our sins are taken care of."

"Yes!" I loved the picture in my mind. I understood. "It's what I'd been longing for. I see it in you, Lois. And in Marsha. What do I do now?"

Lois opened her Bible and pointed to a verse on the page. "You may have heard it before. It's John three-sixteen." She read the verse to me about God loving the world so much "that He gave His only begotten Son, that whosoever believeth in Him should not perish, but have everlasting life."

"James and I had left our destiny to chance. We'd left it in the hands of what we called fate. But it didn't produce any lasting peace. It was fun for the moment, but in the end, it made little sense. I was up for the adventures we've been on, but everywhere we moved, I was searching, not knowing what I was looking for but wanting to build a legacy for my girls."

"Sharon?" Lois asked as she folded her Bible. "Would you like to ask Jesus now to be your Savior and know without a doubt that you'll be with Him forever?"

"I would," I answered.

It wasn't chance that had taken us to Fairbanks or given us our girls or moved us to Bethel, where we met Marsha and Howard. Nor had we just happened to meet Lois and Tom or attend church where we heard Fred share the truth of the gospel. God had been doing His will all along.

Lois took my hand and led me in prayer, and I talked to God and invited Him into my life. I was done taking chances in life. I wanted the peace of God to rule my heart. I couldn't wait to share it with James and my girls, and together, we could know our destiny and purpose.

THAT EVENING, I PULLED OUT MY SONNET OF SAD. I dug around for the journal in my things and shouted out loud when I found it.

"It's here!"

James gave me a queer look.

I reread the sonnet to myself.

PROBLEM

My face doesn't hide how I feel: sad.
Is there an unseen foe?
I've tilled the soil of my soul to grow.
There's no claim I've somehow been bad.
I yearn and toil for my heart to be glad.
Is there a way to know?
For my eternal destiny to show?
It's not a rhyme I seek, or a fad.

. . .

Chapter 30

THAT'S WHERE I'D LEFT OFF ALL THOSE YEARS AGO. Now I had the next part to write. I wrote it down with ease as it flowed from me.

SOLUTION
 I searched and became aware.
 You showed me You are the way.
 All I had to do was admit and pray
 I knew You were there.
 Draw close to me today.
 Thank you that You stay
 And forever that You care.

I TUCKED MY JOURNAL INTO MY TOTE TO SHOW LOIS over the weekend. I got into bed and put my cold feet on James' shins.

"Oh, I love it when you do that. I'm so happy when you get to steal heat from me. And how is it possible that your toes are colder than room temperature?" James said and tapped the tip of my nose with his fingertip.

"James?" I asked.

"Yes, sweets."

"Today, something happened."

James jolted, and my foot slipped off his leg. "What?"

Aha, I'd played him into my hands this time. "I found something."

"C'mon, stop playing. What was it? My football key chain?"

I laughed. "Nope."

"Sheesh, Sharon. My paperclip collection?"

"Nope."

"Is it...my lucky pocket watch?"

"Wow, you're missing a lot of stuff!" I said, happy with my efforts to string him along. "Nope, not a watch."

"Tell me," he pleaded.

"Oh, okay. Today I found what I've been looking for all these years."

"Me!" he said with enthusiasm. "But Sharon, I've been here all along." He pretended to pry my eyes open with his fingertips.

"Nope, not you either, James. Today, when I went with Lois to church, I prayed and asked God to forgive me of my sins and be my Savior. Today, I became a part of the family of God, and I'm so excited!" I rolled over onto my back. "It changes everything, James."

"Really?" he questioned and leaned up on one elbow, facing me.

"Yup, it does. More than anything, I want the same for you and the girls. Can I tell you more?"

"Yes, Sharon, I'm willing to take a chance on you."

"That's it though, James, no more chances, no more games. It's about trusting and having faith."

We talked into the night hours, and I prayed silently to myself for James to understand so that he wouldn't chance his life on a whim, but trust in the God of Chances, the God who'd ruled the dice and the numbers from the very beginning.

EPILOGUE

I FLIPPED THROUGH THE SCRAPBOOK ON MY LAP AS I sat next to my granddaughter, Christine.

"Grandma, how many times did you move?" she asked.

"I lost track, my dear. Your grandpa and I did a duo almost every year where he worked customs in one location for the summer and was a teacher during the school year. We finally settled here in Tok, thank God. We bought this house and raised your mom, Auntie Roberta, and Sam."

As I answered Christine, I looked at her fine features and thought about how much she resembled her mom, Brooke.

It didn't seem possible that we would be hosting dozens of family members for Christine's wedding day the very next day. She was marrying a childhood friend, a high school sweetheart, and now the love of her life.

"Moving around so much didn't really matter, though. Once I found out what it meant to have a personal relationship with Jesus, everything changed."

"I regret not asking more questions, Grandma. I didn't know there was ever a time you didn't have Him in your life." She set the scrapbook down on the coffee table.

"I was saved after many circumstances came together and I'd

read a book that explained the gospel clearly. I also saw joy and peace in the Christians I knew, and I wanted the peace they had. A few months later, your grandpa accepted Christ with Fred at his side."

"Grandpa wasn't a Christian either?" She looked at me in awe. "He's one of the most dynamic people I know. His servant's heart, always helping people..."

"He's always been like that, such a goodie, and it's what made it harder for him to acknowledge he needed a savior. He kept his feelings inside for a while and then opened up when he saw the peace transform me from the inside out. By the way, your grandpa and I have an early gift for you, Christine." I reached beside the couch and pulled out a bright-blue bag with yellow tissue tucked in the top. "Go ahead, open it now," I said, eager to see her response.

"Sure, Grandma." Christine removed the tissue and pulled out the item I'd tucked inside.

She held the gift out in front of her. "Grandma! It's the same cross-stitched verse you have in your house on your mantel."

"Yes, honey. It was one of our wedding gifts. Shortly after we opened the gift, I'd tucked it away and boxed it up, not knowing what a treasure it was. If only we'd known the truth. Our prayer is that you'll use the wisdom of the verse in your marriage. Trust in Him"—I paused and pointed upwards—"and He will direct all your paths. Believe me, it's much better than rolling the dice and hoping for the best."

"Aw, thanks, Grandma. Did you make it?"

"Your grandpa did."

"For real?" Christine asked and leaned closer to me.

"Nope." I laughed. "He'd be cross-eyed. I made it."

Christine reached out her arms, and we hugged. "Love you, Grandma."

"Love you too, sweetie. Now, what time do I have to be at the rehearsal?" I questioned.

"You and Grandpa can be there at noon. Or even earlier, especially since Grandpa is officiating the wedding."

A smile spread across my face. At Christine's wedding, there would be four generations of Klines. Mary had arrived yesterday for the festivities, and so had another granddaughter and her baby girl.

"Okay, dear, we'll be there." I stood up and felt my hips tighten as did. Thankfully, it was summer, and the pains of arthritis didn't bother me much in the warmer temperatures.

As I walked to the door to see Christine off, I saw James out in the yard, watering the flowers. Christine and her husband would take their wedding photos in front of our log home after the ceremony. It was the least we could do to help make the day special.

The tall delphiniums and fireweed stood proud against our log home, and scattered alyssum, bordered with grass, left a sweet aroma in the air. The passing of time was a beautiful reminder of God's faithfulness.

Thank you, LORD, that as we've stood on your promises, You've been our rock and fortress. As we've stood on Your promises, You've blessed us with three children and now many grandchildren about to set out on their own. Thank you, Lord, thank you.

JAMES STOOD AT THE FRONT OF THE CHURCH AND pulled at his necktie. It was a hot July day with the temperature outside in the high eighties. I sat in the pew of Faith Chapel, smiling at him. He was handsome, dressed in his suit with his gray hair and dark complexion. His dark eyes shone with pride as the wedding processional began, and he raised his arms.

"Will you please rise?" he said.

Christine walked down the aisle, her arm clasping her tall father's forearm. I noted the tear in his eye and shot a glance at

Brooke. She beamed and pushed her lips together, probably holding back her emotion as best she could. I remembered the day we gave her away, and now she stood proud of her daughter and her seven other children. One of her daughters was what she called an "adopt-a-daughter" and had come alongside them, and she'd gathered her into the family's fold.

Gulping back tears, I dabbed my eyes with my handkerchief and shifted my position as Christine neared the front of the church. The same church where I'd bowed my heart in prayer and asked for the gift of salvation. Now we bore the fruit of our faith, raising our children in the way they should go, and they'd chosen to follow the legacy we'd taught them of faith in Christ.

Roberta stood behind Brooke's family. All of her seven children traveled from across the country to attend the summer wedding. Two of her kids were already married with children of their own. Our son, Sam, stood among them with his wife and their two teen boys. Most of the witnesses of the wedding were our family. The rest were our church family at Faith Chapel.

"Who gives this lovely young lady to be married to this guy?" James said and gave Christine a wink.

"Her...her mother and I do." Christine's dad seemed to push the words out. They were hard to say.

Relinquishing your children was one of the hardest things to do as a parent. I nodded at Brooke and smiled as she gave Christine a hug and then sat in the front with her husband.

James spoke up. "You may be seated." He cleared his throat and tucked the Bible in his hand under his arm. "A long time ago, in a faraway land, I married the most beautiful woman in the world." James smiled at me. "We thought we were in love, and that we'd never love each other more than we did that day." He reached his hand to his face and wiped a tear from his eye. "You might not believe me, but I love my wife more today than I ever have. Love grows and grows." He looked between Christine and her soon-to-be-husband. "However, way back then, we were missing an ingredient in our marriage. We did not have Christ as the center. I am here to tell you today that it made all the difference in the world once we did. We had a firm foundation. We allowed the living Word of God to prevail in our home. Sharon and I trusted in God to be our all in all, and it changed us forever.

"Christine and Jared, I encourage you to do the same. Don't watch me too closely because I'm fallible, but watch the family around you and notice how they bring Christ into their marriages. May God bless you in your obedience to Him." James paused and looked over to me, and we smiled at one another. He mouthed, *I love you.*

I felt the heat rise to my face, and I beamed at James and whispered, "I love you too." And I loved him more than ever as well, and it was because God's love was in me shining through.

God, our Alaskan chance brought us to You and I will be forever grateful for all the chances you put before me to draw me unto Yourself. In turn, my faith is now invested in the generations to come. You are an awesome God.

*WAIT...BEFORE YOU GO WILL YOU DO ME A FAVOR? WILL YOU TAKE **the time to write a review for me on the Goodreads? Just a few words of how the story resonated with you.***
   https://www.goodreads.com/book/show/60282072-alaska-chance
   Also head on over to my website at
   https://mary-ann-landers.com and subscribe to my newsletter to stay in the loop.

ACKNOWLEDGMENTS

I'd like to thank my husband and three kids for their *amazing* help in my writing. The assistance with ideas, words, edits and phrases is a huge help to this Canada born gal trying to make sense of differences in spelling and phrases.

Together we've survived vehicles breaking down at -40F in the middle of Fairbanks and then top it off with a morning temperature reading of -70F a couple of weeks later.

Thank you to my extended family; Dromarsky's, Landers, Millers, Andersons, Paulsons and Sterlings for all your love and support. A big high five to my young nieces for all your feedback because when you quote my books it warms my heart!

I also have the *bestest* writing group here in Tok with Sara, Shelly and Jodi. Thanks gals for nudging me along, laughing and crying with me each step of the way.

ABOUT THE AUTHOR

Alaskan based author Maryann Landers writes women's faith filled fiction based on true stories of extraordinary women of her magnificent state. She loves to showcase the unique north and give her readers a little taste of rustic Alaska.

While writing in her log home in the woods she is also looking forward to her next adventure with her Alaskan husband, juggling mom tasks such as crafting homemade meals from moose and caribou meat, building DIY projects from scrap wood piles and guiding her teens in their homeschooling.

To learn about her inspiration to write Alaskan based stories read her blog at www.mary-ann-landers.com

Her first novel in the Alaskan Women of Caliber Series; **Alaskan Calibration** released June 2021 followed by **Alaska Calling** in September, 2021.

ALSO BY MARYANN LANDERS

Alaskan Women of Caliber Series:

Book 1: Alaskan Calibration

Book 2: Alaska Calling

Book3: Alaska Chance

Book 4: Alaskan Escape - Coming October 2022

For vendors visit:

https://mary-ann-landers.com

Made in the USA
Middletown, DE
24 October 2022